Honey

Honey

A NOVEL

BRENDA BROOKS

Published by ECW Press
665 Gerrard Street East
Toronto, Ontario, Canada M4M 1Y2
416-694-3348 / info@ecwpress.com

Editor for the press: Jennifer Knoch
Cover design: Natalie Olsen / Kisscut Design
Cover photo: © Jen Squires /
www.jensquiresphotographer.com
Author photo: Shari Macdonald

LIBRARY AND ARCHIVES CANADA CATALOGUING
IN PUBLICATION

Title: Honey : a novel / Brenda Brooks.

Names: Brooks, Brenda, 1952– author.

Identifiers: Canadiana (print) 20190114037
Canadiana (ebook) 20190114045

ISBN 9781770414976 (softcover)
ISBN 9781773054018 (PDF)
ISBN 9781773054001 (EPUB)

Classification: LCC PS8553.R656 H66 2019
DDC C813/.54—dc23

The publication of *Honey* has been generously supported by the Canada Council for the Arts which last
year invested $153 million to bring the arts to Canadians throughout the country and is funded in part
by the Government of Canada. *Nous remercions le Conseil des arts du Canada de son soutien. L'an dernier,
le Conseil a investi 153 millions de dollars pour mettre de l'art dans la vie des Canadiennes et des Canadiens de
tout le pays. Ce livre est financé en partie par le gouvernement du Canada.* We acknowledge the support of
the Ontario Arts Council (OAC), an agency of the Government of Ontario, which last year funded 1,737
individual artists and 1,095 organizations in 223 communities across Ontario for a total of $52.1 million. We
also acknowledge the contribution of the Government of Ontario through the Ontario Book Publishing
Tax Credit, and through Ontario Creates for the marketing of this book.

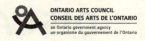

PRINTED AND BOUND IN CANADA   PRINTING: FRIESENS   5   4   3   2   1

For my sister

I Remember

By the first of August
the invisible beetles began
to snore and the grass was
as tough as hemp and was
no color — no more than
the sand was a color and
we had worn our bare feet
bare since the twentieth
of June and there were times
we forgot to wind up your
alarm clock and some nights
we took our gin warm and neat
from old jelly glasses while
the sun blew out of sight
like a red picture hat and
one day I tied my hair back
with a ribbon and you said
that I looked almost like
a puritan lady and what
I remember best is that
the door to your room was
the door to mine.

— *Anne Sexton*

Part I

This is the girl.
> — *Mulholland Drive*

I NEVER WENT BACK TO the house on Montague Street again. I didn't even return to town. The day of my release I thought about dropping by Robinson's on 3rd to pick up something new to wear, give myself the illusion of a fresh start, that sort of thing, but there were bound to be a few locals around who remembered what happened so I kept driving.

All I took with me was a suitcase and that thrift store hourglass Honey gave me on Christmas Eve, the night before they ran off: brass with genuine hand-blown bulbs. She said it was precise, never got clogged, the sand always ran true. It turned out to be symbolic as hell but that's the nature of an hourglass after all: it whispers the bottom line without saying a word.

No, I never returned to Buckthorn at all. It would have been like cruising through an abandoned movie set, tumbleweeds blowing down the boulevard, the last fake storefront nailed shut — which is what that godforsaken place was bound for anyway. That's why you've never heard of my hometown; it doesn't exist anymore, at least not in the way I remember. Maybe it never did. Look at me, will you: twenty-five and already living in the past.

Honey was from Buckthorn too, although from childhood on she bullshitted about various far-flung locales being her true birthplace. I went along for the fun of it. And after all, our town being what it was, who could blame her for getting stoned now and then and dreaming? Elba, some island in Italy, was her favorite fantasy. She had a thing about it for years. According to her she'd been born there in another life. The life that counts, she said. I sometimes thought she would have chosen any exotic locale as long as it had a beach, a big red sunset, and rose-colored sand. Sand that color is pretty unlikely, I told her, even in Elba, but that didn't bother her. She liked pretty unlikely things, her dreams (and old scrapbooks) full of beaches and ruins and views of sparkling seas through open windows — things like that. In a way I guess you could say that this whole mess came down to Honey trying to find her true-blue homeland. And me doing my best not to lose her again.

I'm not much for talking, now more than ever, although I'm sure that's hard to believe. I mean, look at me rattling on. If you ask me where I'm from, what it was like there, or what I mean by what happened, I'll tell you about Honey. Because she's where I'm from, and the only place I've ever really been.

She's what happened.

I.

I OPENED WITH THE SAME song every night, because it got me in the mood, took me away. A few bars into Nat King Cole's "Unforgettable," and I wasn't stuck in some stinking casino behind the Walmart on the outskirts of Buckthorn anymore. In my imagination it was just me and the piano on a revolving dais in a swank venue. Slick tuxes, formal gowns, martinis, and beautiful people who never had to worry about how much cash they set aside for retirement. A room with a crystal chandelier. Why not? It was nothing like reality. So then a bit of tenor sax, silky strings, a touch of that easy legato brushwork on percussion.

Picture me and the baby grand as seen from above, the room tinted deep purple, a spray of light revolving over the walls and ceiling. I don't mean a hokey disco ball kind of thing. I'm talking about true darkness, slivers of light stolen from the stars, and glittering throughout, as if me and the Steinway were our own little planet turning slowly in space. White shirt, black skirt. The camera would pan across my hands, which I'm told are both strong and graceful, if a little pale.

The piano is the only place my hands feel at home, the only time, between you and me, when they know precisely what they're doing. Because they know "Unforgettable." And for a while so do the gamblers and losers, along with tunes like "Body and Soul," "Stardust," and "Unchained Melody" — balm for the poor, or about to be, in the penniless twilight hours. My delivery isn't velvet like Nat's. I'm a bit hoarse to tell the truth, my voice raw from a bout of childhood strep that never quite resolved. But I can sing, rise above myself when I'm taken away, even if the pipes aren't necessarily grand enough to elevate the assembled. *No never before, has someone been more . . .*

I'd barely had time to conclude my fantasy set that night when Eddie, the casino manager, touched my shoulder and slipped a note under my tips glass: *urgent phone call.* I had to smile, because the whole thing suggested one of those old thrillers Honey and I watched as kids while her mother lay passed out in the easy chair and we finished her glass of rum. You'd think I'd watched enough of those old gems to know that a gesture like Eddie's, especially in a setting like the Crescendo Casino, had to be portentous. That's how I got the news about my father, how I came to stand by his grave a little over a year ago, hoping my mother would stay in her coma until I found the words to tell her that the accident she survived had killed him.

He died trapped in a beat-up Volvo under the Scarlet River Bridge, Buckthorn County's one and only scenic landmark. My mother had forgotten to fasten her seatbelt and floated free — ironic, I know.

A few days after the accident I went down to the drugstore and bought the last of the Scarlet River Bridge postcards, which had been hanging around on that rickety wire rack since I was twelve, took them home, lit my father's hibachi, and burned them one at a time while I stood on the patio drinking the last of his beer. It's not that I had anything against the bridge (it was the drunk in the Jeep who killed him), I just needed to *do* something, as Honey's mother, Inez, used to say when things got too quiet.

I didn't have to be right there with him in the Volvo that day to know that my father had cinched his seatbelt tight before slipping the key into the ignition. He was as consistent as the metronome perched on the family piano: he never cheated on his taxes; his music classes ended at five; his tie, when he wore one, matched his shirt and sometimes his socks; there were gloves in his glove compartment year-round — and, no, he never failed to fasten his seatbelt, so he sank beneath the waves stuck inside what may as well have been a 3,000-pound stone. And all of this because of a drunk guy in a Jeep with a cell phone. But then a bit of serendipity softened the horrible luck: a woman passing by on a mountain bike pulled my mother to shore by her hair.

How were things supposed to end for my father? The way I'd imagined all along, of course: many years down the road and him toppled by a gust of wind at ninety-two, and then a blissful period spent stuffed with fantastic drugs and wrapped snug in the old La-Z-Boy, my mother standing by. And me, child prodigy turned middle-aged (by then) pie-ano player, fulfilling his last musical requests.

He'd say something like, "Well, kid, how about you crack the lid on that battered baby grand" — it was a beat-up Baldwin — "for your old man's last night here on Earth? Don't forget to keep an eye on your tempo. More pulse, less rubato is what I think we're after in times like these." Then he'd suggest something in dark green, as if songs could be chosen like a new suit. We'd carry on with our regular give and take about what to play, and then I'd get on with the same two pieces I played most nights until I left home, bliss all over his face straight through to the end: Chopin Nocturne Op. 9 No. 2 and Burt Bacharach's "Walk on By." I'd fold my hands into my lap, look up, and he'd be gone — except for the peaceful countenance, which would have gone unshaven for a month, making him look, just for a moment, like Verdi.

Yes, that's the way it would have unfolded on the big screen if I'd been the director of the movie about my father's life. As it turns out, I'm nothing more than a piano player on the soundtrack.

That crappy description of myself would have ticked my mother off, because she wouldn't have been able to help seeing the truth in it. My long-ago Saturday morning miracle — when I'd scrambled onto the piano bench at four years old and knocked out a copy of some corny concerto meandering along behind the cartoons — was too long gone to recall, unless you were my mother who, for a therapist, seemed to have an awful hard time letting go of things. Maybe it was true I lacked ambition. I'd squandered my gifts. All those piano lessons, music camps, and trips to recitals;

the write-ups in the papers about the musical prodigy from poor, faltering Buckthorn County had come to nothing but late-night shifts at the Crescendo Casino out on Highway 7.

It wasn't bragging rights my mother wanted. She would have found those baby Beethovens on YouTube as creepy as I did, if she'd watched them. I'm not even sure the lost loot played on her mind, except that it reduced the possibility of a comfortable future outside of our good old horrible hometown, as Honey called it. I knew where my mother's heartache lay because I saw her face whenever I gave in and played something legit especially for her: that look of dreamy delight torn in half by the knowledge that sooner or later I'd snap on those cheesy dollar sign cufflinks and croon pop songs for a bunch of drinkers and gamblers.

After my father's funeral service a couple of friends offered to take me to lunch — people who felt sorry for me, let's be honest, because I had no close friends. Most of the people I grew up with had left for the city or fled even farther afield in search of work. On top of that I had always been a socially inept little geek who, when she wasn't hunched over the piano keyboard, limited her attention to the one friend who mattered — the one true-blue pal who had flown the coop. And, at twenty-four, the piano was my oldest friend. I was like a postulant who married the church, except I'd committed myself to a no-nonsense, clerical Baldwin (it really did look a bit like a squat parson) and carried on an intense flirtation with a beguiling Steinway concert grand (Model D, ebony finish, 1980!) — forty-five minutes of fingertip bliss at Frederick's Piano Emporium whenever I drove down to the city.

My father's two remaining brothers and their wives came from Saskatchewan to visit my mother in the hospital and attend the funeral. After they headed back to the airport hotel I found two envelopes with $500 each in my car, unlabeled but I knew who had left them. My mother had no siblings. "She's one of a kind," as my father always said. And any extended family had stayed in Scotland — distant relations, you could say, who I notified and promised to keep updated though I knew my mother hadn't been in touch for years.

You'd think the reality of my dead father and comatose mother would have numbed my brain, but the constant worry about money elbowed its way back in as I turned from the grave. My mother's prognosis was good, but what if the expected insurance payout didn't come through and she couldn't carry on with her counselling practice for an extended period? How would she make do without the money my father brought in with his music lessons and the pittance I might contribute by squandering my talent? I barely had enough to pay the rent at my apartment over Vesuvius Pizza.

In 2008 my parents lost everything but the house and cars (my mother's Volvo now ruined by the river) and, like everyone else in Buckthorn, resigned themselves to working right up to the edge of the forced retirement waiting down the road for all of us, as my father might have put it. And who knew better now than him?

I thought I might pick up some work at the casino outside of my evening hours playing covers in the lounge. I could learn to be a croupier, as Honey had once, though I sucked at games of all kinds. Maybe a job in retail, maybe, maybe, maybe . . . but then I ran out of maybes because there hadn't been any jobs in Buckthorn since the tomato plant closed in 2012 and most of the retail had since followed suit. That was the reason for the county pit, a dumping ground for garbage from the city, and the windmills turning in the farm fields all the way down to Torrent.

After the service I intended to go straight home and sort through our new problems — spread things out on the kitchen table and stare, scribble, crunch numbers until I convinced myself the insurance policy would solve everything and I wouldn't have to tell my mother that her beloved guy was lost to the river and her cherished house to the bank. Otherwise, how long would I have to go on hoping she stayed unconscious?

I had just let the full impact of that twisted hope hit me when I saw the old Eldorado parked by the cemetery gates and Honey standing next to it.

Six years had passed since I last saw her, since she and her mother had left town when we were both eighteen — and nothing since. They left on Christmas Day but had shown up for Christmas Eve as usual.

All day a good old Buckthorn squall had torn away at the trees along the avenue, branches shattered and strewn about the yard. By the time the storm died down four feet of new snow had fallen and the power had gone out twice. My father shoveled the walk every hour or so for our two guests, who were renowned for arriving suddenly and late. My mother had given up on the oven, fired up the barbecue, and finished the turkey out on the patio, bundled up in her coat and scarf.

"Here come the girls from Ipanema," my father said as the Caddy turned the corner at Duvalle and came storming up the boulevard. Snow and exhaust fumes billowed behind as it charged around the corner at Montague and slid to a stop at the top of our drive. Later, after the party was over and they sped away again, tires whining on the hardpack, it would look as if someone had discharged a musket full of birdshot into the charred snow behind the tailpipe.

Honey and her mother waltzed in with a basket of martini fixings — olives, onions, swizzle sticks Inez had swiped from the local pub, a jumbo bottle of gin, of course — and a six-pack of Dos Equis for my father because Honey's mother had read somewhere that Janis Joplin loved the stuff and that seemed to cinch its value as a "loosener-upper," which Inez thought my father needed. Not that he didn't know how to have a good time. He'd grown up on the Prairies with a pile of siblings accustomed to big, noisy holidays and everyone torturing "O Holy Night" and spilling liquor on the piano, so when "the girls" burst through the door with a bunch of CDs (Herb Alpert, Astrud Gilberto, a little disco, the Supremes) and cocktails, he was delighted to toss away the metronome, so to speak, and do some improvising.

My folks invited Honey and Inez for most special occasions — Thanksgiving, Christmas, birthdays, since Honey and I were born the same day — ever since Honey's father, the pro at the local golf course, had gone AWOL. My mother didn't have much use for Mr. Ramone, and I assumed this was because she had sensed a few significant drawbacks regarding the couple's marriage. At least, that's how she would have put it, in that therapeutic lingo of hers. Not that anyone in town could have missed the patrol car often parked in front of the Ramones' duplex on the weekend.

I once overheard my mother mutter to my father that Al Ramone wasn't so much a golfer as a guy who liked to get smashed at the golf course after aerating the greens with his spikes. My mother could be indignant, and sharp, at times. But to be fair, these weren't her only sides. She had nothing but compassion for her clients — all those drug problems and broken marriages and wild children — not that she ever breathed a word about what went on behind closed doors. As a kid, all I ever heard were low murmurs and sighs, soft as the sound reeds make when they slip past the sides of a canoe. And the crying.

The Christmas Honey and her mother left town for good went like semi-inebriated clockwork: turkey dinner washed down with a bottle of Blue Nun, and then out came the fruitcake and shortbread and I played "O Tannenbaum" in my best Vince Guaraldi style while my father joked with Inez and my mother steamed the plum pudding. Honey and I exchanged gifts: she gave me the hourglass and I gave her a blue scarf. My gift seemed boring in comparison but I'd spent a lot of time picking it out, layering on all sorts of meanings, like I'd torn a piece out of the sky, or somehow bought her a river.

After things were cleared away Inez read my mother's tea leaves. She always began the same way — "Oh, now this is interesting" — and turned the cup this way and that in her beautiful hands, which were offset with southwest-style bangles and a ring with an amethyst the size of a walnut. Now and then we caught a glimpse of the rose tattoo on her neck, half-hidden by her wild ash-blonde hair. She always found something positive to say about my mother's future, which I thought was kind of her. Honey said she really believed that crap and the only reason she didn't bring her Ouija board was because my mother would freak and throw them out, which we both knew wasn't true. Inez said things like, "The next year will be exciting. Maintain focus in order to juggle work, social life, and healthy practices. Prioritize your well-being." If she saw the real truth — dead husband, lost mind — she kindly kept it to herself.

Later, after it was clear they'd vamoosed for good and stuck us with their ancient dog, Dude, who they left in our backyard with a note tied to his collar — *something's come up! sorry about this! will repay!* — my mother said the tea leaf reading didn't have to be so complicated: "She might have just gone ahead and told me she saw an incontinent Bull Terrier in my future."

After the reading, on that last Christmas Eve, Honey and I had walked back to the duplex on Argyle Avenue to let the dog out for a crap. We hung out for a while under the street lights with the snow coming down and the banks glittering like crushed-up diamonds all along the crescent up to Broad Street. She lit a cigarette, which smelled blue on the cold air, and then tossed the match away, a tiny scribble in the dark. She always let the smoke drift from the side of her mouth like a noir starlet. A hokey line from one of our old movie favorites followed a look like that. I remembered that night's offering for a long time; it was the last I'd hear for a while.

"*Kiss* me. I want you to *kiss* me," she cried. "The liar's kiss that says I *love* you and means something else." I pushed her away, as usual, but not before she singed the tips of my hair with her cigarette. How we laughed, our voices the only sound under the low winter sky. We wandered around another half-hour or so, out to the field across from Duvalle and around the block to have a gawk at the Christmas lights on the boulevard, and then she clipped the leash on the dog and we followed our tracks back to Montague to pick up Inez.

And even though she must have known they were abandoning Buckthorn before daylight, she was silent as the night, this girl I'd known forever who would call me up and go on for hours about some crazy thing her old man did, or about "some asshole" she'd told to fuck off. Sometimes she simply read to me from one of her mother's recipe books, lingering over the culinary notes as if the intricacies of copper pots and pepper mills and wooden spoons and mandolines were some kind of miracle.

That night she didn't say a word about her plans to vanish from our lives; she just slipped her arm through mine and sang a line from that old Joni Mitchell song about wishing she had a river she could skate away on. And I guess something in me faltered, because even though I registered the melody I failed to hear the meaning behind the lyric, which just shows my limitations in playing by ear.

2.

ALL THOSE YEARS. And what's the first thing she says at the cemetery that day? "With my brains and your looks we could go places."
So much like her, and yet not, because she said it softly, not a hint of
the drifter's bravado in *The Postman Always Rings Twice*, one of our
top oldies. Back in the day this would have been my cue to become
the femme fatale and dish something back — but under the circumstances? She blushed, as if the line had slipped out like the old
habit it was. We both looked down. I stared at her hands and saw
her fingers when we were eight, or ten, chipped sparkle polish on
her nails, shuffling cards, fussing with the gears on her bike, lacing
up her hockey skates.

I'm not sure if I met her square in the eyes, but if so it was only
for a moment, and then I looked away again, down at her skinny
jeans blown out at the knees, then up the length of her coat, a dark

wool thrift-store buy, the type we liked as teens. It seemed to me her boots were the pair she wore while tearing up the countryside on some guy's motorcycle back in the day, and me in my flip-flops clinging to her from behind, terrified.

That day was warm for April; I'd removed my steaming blazer at the grave site, but she wore two or three layers underneath the coat — a shirt under a sweater with oversize plastic buttons — and a scarf, green, with crushed tassels.

"Christ, Nic," she said and stared even harder at my shoes. And what was the right response to that tiny chip of a statement after so long a wait? It was almost as though she read my thoughts because she added, "I just — don't know what to say."

"Think of something, will you?" I said, all in a rush, because it's not like the words hadn't been queuing in my throat all those years. I half-forgot my father getting shoveled into the ground behind us. But then she reminded me.

"Shit. I'm so sorry he's gone. I just couldn't believe it when I heard."

She pulled a bunch of damp Kleenex out of her pocket — two or three dropped to the ground. I picked them up, stuffed them back into the pocket of her overcoat, thinking of my father's expression for the balled-up tissues in my mother's wastebasket at the end of her counselling day, all those "white roses of despair."

Another lengthy period of silence followed — a patch of emptiness so profound that I thought it might go on forever, and we'd just continue standing there until our time came and then topple into a nearby grave.

"I'm so goddamn sorry I missed the service," she said.

I laughed. At least, I guess it was a laugh, and I suppose it belonged to me, because her own face remained solemn, drawn.

"Nic, I . . ."

"Let's see if I've got this straight." I said. "You're sorry he's gone, couldn't believe it when you heard the news, and regret you missed the service."

I had to give her credit because she was too proud, if nothing else, to look away. For a few seconds I wasn't sure how to follow up, and then carried on, "And what about my mother?"

"Of *course* your mom. I was going to say . . ."

"You were going to add her to our list of regrets?"

"Of course not. I mean — yes. Oh shit."

I took her in. She looked raw, like someone recovering from an illness. That kind of hollowed-out look about the eyes. I'd just begun thinking of lightening up, giving her a chance — because who knew? Maybe one of the many things I feared really *had* happened, maybe she'd been kidnapped, dug a tunnel to freedom, a mile per year, and came straight back to tell me about it — when she regrouped and got a little testy herself.

"Look, if you want to tear an honest strip off me about something please bring it on. But don't do this other thing, because . . ."

"An honest strip about something?"

She slipped a pair of sunglasses out of her coat and put them on. I would have recognized her mother's old cat-eyes anywhere. But how solemn she looked, and so far away from eighteen, as she turned away from me, the deep green lenses against her pale cheek. She glanced at the Eldorado. I reached out, removed her glasses, and folded them in my hand.

"Don't worry. I won't try to stop you," I said. "Because it's just too hard, isn't it? Dragging yourself back to — what did you always call it? — 'this fucking hellhole of ours.' But the least you can do is look me in the eyes after six goddamn years of nothing. You know, just stand there and — look at me." I considered holding that moment for five or six seconds, then turning and walking away. At least I'd have my dignity, as long as I remembered where I parked the car. On the other hand, this might be my last chance to have it out with her and why squander the moment? So I carried on. "I mean, what did you think I'd say, 'Hey, Honey. Where the heck you been? Sorry I missed your phone calls. How come no recipe tips for the last three thousand days?' Or whatever it's been?"

"Please," she said and reached for the glasses. "I'm sorry for everything — all of it. I know exactly how shitty I've been. There's nothing you could accuse me of that isn't bang on. Name it. Anything. You don't know the half of it."

When I didn't answer she gave up on the glasses and began buttoning her coat. The last button was missing. A few threads clung there and she brushed them away and squared her shoulders.

"Yes, I'll look you in the eye. That's mostly why I came back after all. But I'll tell you what I won't do: I won't play this game."

We both stood our ground, I guess you could say. I wanted to break down and tell her how all this time I thought she must be dead. Didn't she know that? Why else would I stop hearing from someone whose whereabouts I'd known every day of every week since childhood? And now, seeing her standing there, every awful thing I'd imagined came rushing back: she'd drowned in some river, been kidnapped, sold as a sex slave, murdered by some loser driving a van stuffed with torture devices, or — lost forever to a drunk in a Jeep.

"Honestly," she said, "just haul off and slug me. I know I deserve it. But don't torture both of us with this whole passive-aggressive thing."

When I turned to go, she grabbed my sleeve.

"Drive with me," she said.

Rumor had it that the girls from Ipanema had disappeared because Honey got pregnant and Inez dragged her off to get an abortion. But Buckthorn rumors always come in grimy droves. Another was Inez finally went off the deep end and Honey dragged *her* off to the nuthouse to dry out. Everyone seemed to know that Mrs. Ramone's daughter was easy and wild, and Mrs. Ramone herself drank up a storm and grew pot plants in the duplex, although it would have been easier to name someone who didn't drink too much and get high in Buckthorn, outside of my parents. Or some said Honey's often-absent father had robbed a bank somewhere and sent for Honey and Inez, so they said fuck the old furniture and shitty TV and deserted the crappy duplex on Argyle Avenue like anyone in their right mind would. But most people assumed they had stiffed the landlord one too many times, like plenty of others before them, and fled to salvage some dignity.

Inez may have been overdoing it with her migraine medication (washed down with whiskey) but the rest was b.s. Honey had made it through her teen years by taking and borrowing more things from guys than she ever gave away: dirt bikes, motorboats, snow machines, and, later, dinners and tickets to see popular bands in the city. No, she didn't get in trouble because of some guy. With her looks and smarts, there was every chance she'd make the right connections and score a hot job in the city someday.

I just couldn't understand what came over them to disappear so suddenly, or why she never contacted me. All my emails bouncing back? The canceled phone? Hadn't I proven myself to be an ace confidante? Who held the pail while she siphoned gas for the ravenous Eldorado? Who else could she have trusted to keep it zipped when she found that rusty pistol tucked inside a battered suitcase behind the abandoned Shell station? We were fourteen or fifteen by then. Not that she needed to worry, because Inez, when she discovered the gun, stuffed it into a Corn Flakes box and pushed it to the back of the shelf. "It's probably lost its bang," she said. "But might come in handy for a prop someday."

The afternoon she appeared at Buckthorn Cemetery, Honey may have looked depleted from wherever her travels had taken her, but she still knew how to swing that boat around on a dime and make tracks down the highway. I studied the inside of the car as she drove: tuner knob missing, the steering wheel worn smooth over god knows how many miles — impossible to say how many because the mileage meter, like the clock, had been buggered, as her mother put it, from the get-go. A bunch of Inez's old cassettes lay scattered across the dash. Stacks of clothing, neatly folded, hid the back seat, and on the floor were a couple of picnic coolers and three or four plastic water jugs. Shirts and sweaters on hangers hung from the windows. I ached to know the lay of the land, but her proud bearing held me back. All in good time, I figured.

The so-called vintage Eldorado had been pretty much a beautiful wreck right from the day she and Inez came cruising down the avenue and parked in front of our place on Montague Street. Inez listed the car's stats for my father while he circled the beast several times: phantom gray, genuine leather upholstery, top-of-the-line everything.

"It's been around the block but pretty damned swish, wouldn't you say?" Inez said, as she fired up a Player's Light. She said the car had spent its whole life in Austin, Texas, and did we know that it was sunny in Austin, Texas, 228 days of the year and hadn't snowed for thirty-five years? She wished they would have left the Texas plates on the car but the authorities wouldn't permit it.

She pointed out what the manual called the "vestigial fins and aggressive grill" while Honey slipped behind the wheel and I gazed down the length of the beast. Yes, it was only a car (as my mother pointed out later), but it looked like something that flew to the stars, or hunted along a coral reef, with a body like a long sheet of molten silver and streaked with soft creases, as if someone had gone over it with an iron while it was cooling. It was a week before either of them noticed the clock was forever stuck at 2:03. Later, when things began to drop off or fall apart, Inez called it the Mobster, and Honey joked about the screwed-up wiring that turned the air conditioner on and off at will. When Inez insisted it was the equivalent of owning 350 racehorses, Honey said it was more like having one old nag. Still, a Cadillac Eldorado in any condition was hard to resist at seventeen. Whenever Honey did that clucking sound that kick-starts a horse I knew we were going somewhere. As soon as we left the cemetery that day, I knew exactly where we were going.

I seldom made that drive anymore, but I could have gotten there blindfolded. I mean it: the exit onto Highway 4, ten minutes or so to County Rd. 8, the right turn at the octagonal barn, and then right again at the sign for Crystal Lake and down the gravel road toward the cabins, bait shop, and the boat launch straight ahead. There was a time Honey would hit the gas as if to charge straight over the launch and into the drink, but that day she slowed, turned left before the cabins, and then down a smaller road to the lookout. We parked next to a kiosk where a new sign, already covered with graffiti, offered up a few details about the Buckthorn County area: marine species, wild life, nature of the woodlands — an attempt to promote a little tourism in the area as business declined.

When she turned off the ignition there was nothing but the sound of the wind and waves as they curled into whitecaps and raced toward the beach. The old familiar view rose up: the long row of trees across the opposite shore and the pale blue hills behind.

She rested her hands on the steering wheel, her eyes focused ahead as though we were still driving and if she let go we'd careen off the road. She started right in apologizing again.

"I really *am* sorry, you know."

"I don't want regrets," I said. "I want a story, and a damn good one. So come on, because I've got to get back."

She turned to face me, her knee against the back of the seat, like when we sat eating pizza and bullshitting in the old days.

"Do you remember when we were fifteen — that day the storage locker slammed closed on my arm and busted it? Well, that story was just that: a *story*, a pile of crap." She reached over, snapped open the glove compartment, and fished out a small, silver flask from under a stack of tattered napkins, unscrewed the cap, and offered it to me. I waved it away. I guess she saw something on my face because she assured me that she never took a drink before noon and gestured toward the clock. "And it's three minutes after two, as always, so . . . cheers." She took a couple of sips, screwed the cap back on, and smiled. "Remember how I swilled whiskey while paddling the lake? And yet I still managed to paddle the straight and narrow." She waited for me to go along with her, get in the spirit, but I just wasn't there.

"Wrong story," I said.

"Okay then. But the whole thing's so goddamn embarrassing I can't stand talking about it, which is just one of the many reasons why I never did. The truth is — I broke my arm at the storage locker, sure, but with a little help from the old man. The door itself was completely innocent, an unwilling accessory at most, nowhere else to go." She smiled at this and then told me not to look so shocked, because the cops had been hauling her father off to jail for one reason or another for years.

"You knew that," she said. Sure I did. Sometimes when she called me late at night I could hear Inez and Honey's father going at it in the background, the sounds of things being thrown around, the music turned up, as if that would fool the folks on the other side of the duplex into thinking the battle was really a celebration. But this kind of thing had become almost standard for most of Buckthorn, hadn't it?

"You're telling me your dad broke your arm."

"Here's the facts," she said, serious now. "And this is one-time only, because I owe it to you. And you've got no idea how much I regret not coming clean, and making it right, until so late in the game. If I'm even making it right at all. Because that's up to you." She slipped the flask under her thigh.

"It was a Sunday. The asshole was on a mission to ditch all the shit Inez couldn't *bear* to get rid of and save the locker's storage costs. You know, so he could go on losing golf balls on the fairway and swilling beer in the clubhouse — and god knows what else — rather than get a real job. Half the stuff in the locker was his own crap, but whatever, it had to be done. But then the prick said something about Inez. Something that a father should never say to his daughter about her own mother. I slugged him. Actually broke a finger before the arm; had to tape it later. He grabbed me. We fought like a couple of movie cowboys in a saloon. It's true the locker was mostly full of the kind of shit my mother couldn't resist buying at lawn sales and thrift stores: ornate mirrors, a pair of garish tufted chairs that even a cat had clearly hated, old bottles, stupid pictures in gaudy frames. But so what? Not enough room for his pricey golf clubs, I guess, and those two trophies he won, probably for boozing. He grabbed my arms and pushed me against a bookcase cluttered with all those trinkets that Inez was so wild about." She laughed again. "I can tell you it's really something to find yourself staring into the eyes of an Elvis bust while dear old dad presses himself up against you and goes caveman."

She frowned and took another swig from the flask. "It's not as if that was the first time something bad happened. He'd never broken anything before, that's all. Because I was quick and not usually trapped in a fucking cave with him. And why I never told you is because of the look on your face right now."

"But . . . what do you mean, exactly, by 'goes caveman'?"

She stared at the information sign on the kiosk. Enough time went by that she might have read the entire thing — *Who's Who in the Hinterland* and all the species of fish, and the details about the purple loosestrife invasion over at Hermit's Bog, bullfrogs the size of kittens devouring ducklings in the county ponds.

"A lot of things have changed, but some things haven't," she said finally.

"Which means?"

"It's only that, well — you've kept your innocence nicely intact."

"And that's a bad thing?"

"No," she said and touched my hand. I noticed some of her fingernails were broken and torn, her knuckles raw, and I realized she must have been camping out and making bonfires; that's why her hair smelled of smoke. "I like your innocence, or whatever you want to call it. I think you should hang on to it as long as possible." She withdrew her hand and pulled down her sleeve.

"Afterwards I walked out to the main road where some guy I vaguely remembered from one of those summer incarcerations at McDonald's picked me up and drove me to the hospital. Which he may have regretted because I woofed twice on the way. They set my arm, and I called Inez with some bullshit story about what happened and she drove out and fetched me. When we got home the old man wasn't there. He didn't come home that night, or the next. Two weeks went by, and still no sign of the asshole. I figured Inez thought he'd gone off on another binge, because she didn't seem that surprised. But then one morning, about a month later — she was slinging breakfast dishes in the sink and didn't even look at me — she said, 'By the way, he won't be back.' You can imagine my joy. It was like she'd finally found the balls to see through all the lies and *do* something about what the hell was going on in the fucking house."

She took a deep breath. "But then — three years go by, up to that dinner at your folks', and my mother's reading out the Christmas cards. And there's one of those Hallmark things with a big stone two-story house with gables and all bathed in amber and sparkly snow on the lawn. A mailbox stuffed with bullshit gifts, and a house crammed with happy shiny people. It's from him. And his note says something about having a revelation and he wants to come back and everything's going to be peachy. Same old shit as the old days. And I'm sitting there listening to Inez read out this crap, and I think, *Here we go again.* And I just can't take it. My mother can fall for this shit if she wants, but I can't do it anymore. I'd only been staying to bring in some extra dough, so making that kind of decision screwed me up. I know you didn't know this, but between her depression and headaches, and what she might have called 'a touch of drug addiction,' I doubted she'd ever work again. She got some social assistance, but not enough to cover everything. And plus, I didn't want to leave her with Daddy the Fuck-Up." She took another swig from the flask. "And get this. He signs off his sentimental bullshit card with *It's all going to be uphill from here.* He never could get that direction right. So Inez slips the card back into the envelope with that old pushover look on her face. I'd already started planning my exit, going over the map in my head when she stood up, grabbed that old gun down off the Corn Flakes shelf, and told me to start packing. We ate the last real dinner we'd have in weeks at your place, and then we split early in the morning on Christmas Day."

We sat there quiet for a while, listening to the waves wash up and ease out again.

"But why didn't you tell me? You told me every other goddamn detail of your life. Why the hell didn't you come to me with this too? And what's with just disappearing? I mean, six years? I thought we were best friends, that we were ... *something.*"

"That's why I couldn't say anything. Because I would have had to tell you the whole story. And if your mother found out she might have felt it was her duty as a therapist to report it. And maybe it would have been. And then the police would get involved, and the courts. And you know how Inez thought they were bullshit and wouldn't do a thing. She just wanted to start over, and who could blame her? I think she would have killed him if she'd laid eyes on him again. I really do. I planned on getting in touch with you after we figured out what to do. I guess we just never figured it out, and time slips away. I wanted to come back to you with good news, not a shit sob story, like now." She reached over and rattled around in the glove compartment. "I'm going to have to smoke one of these," she said and fished a cigarette out of the pack, lit it, and rolled the window halfway down.

"And honestly? We may not have returned at all if it hadn't been for a certain morning outside some gas bar in the Midwest. We'd stopped for a bite: a couple of stale muffins and some gas for the Caddy. Inez was taking her sweet time in the ladies can while I waited for her in the foyer. And I see this eighteen-wheeler and the driver checking the load. I knew it was him right away because I'd done nothing but study his every move since I was eight, after all, trying to stay three steps ahead. At first I recoiled behind the rack of sunglasses by the doorway, but then as he came around to hoist himself into the cab I stepped outside. And I swear to god it was almost like my mind forced him to turn and look at me. I walked up to him. We stood there staring at each other. I said, 'Speaking of drivers . . . you left your golf clubs at home.' He cracked an uncertain smile. I smiled too, big and faux-sincere. And then I said, 'If you come back, I'll wait until you're asleep and cave your head in with that club the size of a cantaloupe.' He gave me a long look, stepped up into the cab, and headed back onto the highway. I knew we wouldn't see him again."

"Geez-*uz*," I whispered.

"It was lucky that Inez had fucked around in the ladies so long because I'm pretty sure she would have gone Corn Flakes, if you get my gist."

She unscrewed the cap on the flask and offered it to me, out of habit, confident I wouldn't accept. I took a gulp that set my throat on fire and then spread and glowed in my chest. A story like that? I could almost see how a girl might develop a taste for the hard stuff.

On the way back to Buckthorn she told me about a few of the places they'd ended up before eventually heading east. Money was tight and Inez's health went downhill dealing with life on the road. They bought a tent and Coleman stove and headed south where at least some of the traveling could be done on the cheap. She admitted to having ripped off more than one grocery store. "Out of desperation, of course." Sometimes she foraged for fruit and vegetables at the farms and orchards along the highway, all the while pretending the whole thing was a lark for Inez's sake. She tried to keep her mother in the dark about the urgency of things because over the miles she saw her become more and more subdued and started to worry about her state of mind.

"Miles and mind-numbing miles went by without her saying a thing. She just stared out at the prairie, the sagebrush, the prairie, the tumbleweeds, the prairie, the sagebrush — as we drifted by under a big, shiny blue sky. I wasn't sure if it was the monotony of the landscape or if she, if *we*, were doing a mother/daughter losing our minds thing, bound for matching straightjackets or something.

And to say we were broke is an understatement all rolled up in a thousand miles of bullshit, as Inez put it. Now and then I pulled a fast one on certain amenable guys — to buy cigarettes and renew the migraine meds. And, yes, a bottle of bourbon or two. Why start lying now? And, if I leave any of the tawdry details out it's only because they got sucked out the window somewhere along that unrelenting highway."

"But why didn't you at least email or call? Together we would have thought of something. Didn't we always? I would have gladly kept my mother in the dark as long as you wanted. That's all I did in those days, after all, aside from wander up and down the piano — kept a few pathetic secrets from my mother."

"Do tell," she said. I sat looking at her as if I didn't know what she meant, which was more or less true.

"Nothing to report?" she said. "After such excruciating sincerity from me? That hardly seems fair."

"Oh, it isn't. But I'm afraid it's the sad truth. If I recall anything, or something unfolds down the road, you'll be the first to know. So back to you."

She stared at me a bit longer, sort of tongue-in-cheek, and then moved on. "All I can add is that sometimes things don't have the right ending. Life doesn't run along like a movie — that's one thing I found out. If it did, I'd just rewind and do a whole bunch of stuff over again with a more satisfying conclusion."

By the time we got back to Buckthorn it was 4. She still had the 200-mile drive to Torrent and a room she'd booked. "I'll finally be able to unpack" she said with a smile. She drove me back to my car and we sat for a few seconds staring at the clock. 2:03.

"Well, what are you going to do?" I asked. "Are you staying in

Torrent or heading off somewhere else?" I thought about inviting her to crash at my place, at least overnight. I think she may have seen the thought cross my mind, because she started right in assuring me she'd be fine and needed time alone to think. "It's probably time to stop screwing around on the highway and look for a job," she said, and then laughed. "Did I say that out loud?"

Then out of nowhere she apologized for sticking us with the dog. "Dude's dead, I presume?" she said, followed by that droll look we often exchanged before a fantastic bout of maniacal laughter — but we let it go this time.

"Well, yes, Dude's gone," I said. "It's not as if he wasn't a century old when you — when he came to us. You can imagine how much my mother misses him to this day." And then we did allow ourselves a sort of trial laugh after all.

We hugged. "This is so rough — what you've got on your plate. Are you going to be okay?" she asked when she let me go. "Are *we* going to be okay? Can we get together next time I'm in town? I'll want to keep tabs on you."

"So, you're saying I'm actually going to see you again?"

She crossed her heart. "I promise I'll make it hard for you *not* to see me. And I want you to promise me something in return — and this is important, even though I know it's not top of your list right now. Swear you and your mom will get yourselves a real asshole of a lawyer to handle the accident insurance thing, because from what I heard you deserve a payout — big time. Those fucking insurance guys would rather cut their own throats than cough up dough. Believe me, I've known one or two."

After I started the car and pulled away I realized I'd forgotten to ask about Inez, and she hadn't given me her cell number. But when I turned back she and the Eldorado were gone. On the way home I remembered her remark about the dog and had to smile.

"Dude's dead, I presume?" Only Honey could have made me see the kooky humor in something like that.

3.

MY MOTHER WOKE UP four days later with me sitting beside her hospital bed, the bearer of bad tidings I could hardly bear myself.

In the moment, she was stoic as always, more grim than sad, and I half-wondered if somewhere in the depths of dreamland she somehow sensed my father hadn't made it even before I told her — not that I'd ever suggest such a thing because I knew she hated anything that hinted at mystical woo-woo, and so did I.

The first thing she did when we got home was ask me to settle her into the wing chair with a tumbler of my father's single malt and give her an hour to think. So I went away, but only far enough that I could hear and see her through the side window — her face in her hands and a whole unknown side of her wrenching itself into view. Only a grief-stricken woman with Scottish personality disorder could have packed an entire Irish wake into sixty minutes.

I stood there thinking I should go back in and play something for her, Debussy's "Reverie" maybe and not rush it for a change. But did I? An hour later I waltzed back into the house as if I was none the wiser, and in the days to come we got down to the brass tacks of what it would mean to go on without him.

She had always seen clients in an upstairs room accessed by a set of outside stairs, but that would be a stretch for the time being, so we turned the old TV room on the main floor into her new office. The insurance payout looked to be guaranteed, just as Honey thought, what with the car accident being so blatantly vehicular manslaughter. I suggested that in a few months she might retire and we could reconfigure things further: turn the new office into a library, or dancehall. (It was gratifying to see her crack a smile.) But she seemed determined to carry on until her clients became accustomed to the idea of her retiring — sometime down the road. I pretended not to know that "sometime down the road" meant she had no intention of ever giving up her work. Her clients relied on her too much, and it wasn't as if there would be a shortage of people losing their shit in the next decade the way things were going in the world. On top of that she wanted to keep busy and, I suppose, try to fill the absence my father left behind.

Ours was the last house at the end of a quiet crescent, a brick Victorian ruin on a large lot that my parents had owned since they got married, a monster with gables and windows all over the place, a huge dining area, and four bedrooms upstairs. Mine was in the back overlooking a yard divided into a wildflower garden on the right and vegetable enclosure on the left, and then a patch of grass to pitch a summer tent and, farther on, a few yards of rickety interlocking brick for the barbecue to sit on. There were two century-old maples in the back and a group of three birches whose leaves became a haze of silver in the wind and sounded delicate as the breeze blowing past a guitar somebody left on the porch.

All of this sounds opulent, and it probably had been when the doctor who built the house lived there. But that had been over a century ago and a lot had happened since. The owners before my parents had covered the original siding with cedar paneling that had weathered into gray and begun splintering off here and there, revealing the pink brick and crumbling mortar underneath, like blood and viscera. My parents hadn't been able to afford many improvements themselves. A music teacher and self-employed therapist only had so much extra money for renovations, and none to spare if things went sideways. They had considered selling and even met with a real estate agent, who told them the value was in the double lot and the house was a teardown. They could sell and have money to burn if they moved to a condo in Torrent. My father left the decision to my mother, who said she'd rather go on planting vegetables for another season or two and enjoying a glass of Chardonnay while my father burned something on the grill. She hated the wood siding on the house but always said, "Better that than seeing it turned into dining tables for sale at Pottery Barn."

Two weeks later I threw a few things into a suitcase and moved from my flat over Vesuvius Pizza back to the house, just until she regained her strength, although I could see she was well on her way. And so mother and daughter became roommates, but of course that's laughable in a repressed and dour sort of way. A mother and daughter, no matter what they become, will always be mother and daughter, especially with a river of Scottish blood running through their veins.

Example: in some people's kitchens the breakfast problems begin when somebody burns the toast, and then you have two choices: scrape off the char, or pop another piece in the toaster and get on with your short, precious life. Not in my mother's kitchen though, and I'd forgotten how true this was in the years since I moved out. She liked her toast burned to carbon around the edges and left sitting in the toaster for twenty minutes before starting the egg, which should be poached until the yoke's center was semi-soft while the white itself was ultra-firm. And only when the egg had lingered awhile on the plate should the incinerated toast be buttered (the sound of someone wiping their shoes on a coarse mat) all over the surface, not just in the middle, like some lazy daughters tried to get away with. I'd like to skip right over the part about the tea, but I can't because it's vital: the hot pot, the milk in the cup first, the one-quarter teaspoon of sugar, and so on. By the end of the second week she made her own breakfast, but at lunch I burned the grilled cheese — all the breakfast rules reversed.

At dinner we each took to having a glass of wine, though I'd seldom done so back in my own apartment. A beer on a hot summer day was usually my limit. But I came to require this glass of wine (I began looking forward to it while doing the breakfast dishes) and so did she, whether she knew it or not. Two glasses was pushing it in her view though, so I found myself forgetting things in the kitchen so I could quaff a booster without her knowing. But of course she *did* know, because she was my mother, it's just that she couldn't prove it — and proof is everything.

After dinner she insisted we play Scrabble, which I had always hated but learned to hate more. Honey and I had often played, years before, up at the cabin my parents rented on Serpentine

River for two weeks in the summer. Honey would start things off, on a rainy day, by saying, "Oh F-U-K. It looks like we'll have to play Scarble after all." So we changed the rules to spice things up: Hillbilly Scrabble for instance, with words like yarnt and yawnder and overthar. But then Honey had always mangled spelling on purpose and had been suspended from school once for insisting on spelling god without a capital G, unless it was spelled Gawd. Later we played Dirty Scrabble in our bedroom. She always won, because I was reluctant to spell that kind of thing out, so to speak; she couldn't wait to use every single four-letter word she could think of, which were many, and she happily sacrificed points in order to shock me with just one. So I'd give up and sweep the tiles back into the box. Who really cares who wins at Scarble?

My mother cared. She counted and registered every point, bent over her sheet of paper like an accountant, and smug, like Marley and Scrooge at the takeover meeting. She didn't just win; she proclaimed victory, throwing her hands in the air like a heavyweight boxer or the owner of a thoroughbred who had just won the Triple Crown. But at least her mobility improved, because when you play a board game with that kind of physical abandon you hardly need physical therapy. I took quite a few kitchen breaks while she pondered her next moves.

And we battled on. I don't mean the kind of battles that rocked the neighborhood on Saturday night in Buckthorn (no patrol cars with whirling lights and sirens for us) or gave rise to the kind of outlandish behavior that could be owned up to, rescinded, and forgiven later. What a relief that would have been, but it was probably too Catholic for us. Still, just because you're atheist doesn't mean you can't be Presbyterian too. Battles with my mother had a kind of religious fervor and longevity, the type of silent, drawn-out grudges and disappointments that go on for years. It was as though every Christmas we gave each other the same hair shirt. I doubted she would ever get over my playing piano at the bar in a lousy casino, rather than a fancy concert hall or anywhere else at all. But this all stemmed from her belief that I was a prodigy who had wasted her gifts, when the fact is I never was a prodigy, or virtuoso, or any of those things they called me. I mean, it was Beethoven who wrote the damn thing, not me. I was only a talented piano player (okay, excellent, but it had nothing to do with me) and decent crooner who got paid for entertaining people who had just lost a bundle at blackjack.

But after all, these weren't the best of times. She missed her guy, and I my father, and neither of us knew how to talk about it. Not so strange for tongue-tied me, but I think because of her profession she was frustrated by her inability to make things better through conversation. In the end we handled it this way: if my casino shift permitted it I'd play a few pieces she enjoyed before bedtime (Debussy mostly, never the Chopin or Bacharach, and certainly not that eye-rolling Charles Aznavour song my father sang on her birthday) and she avoided asking me anything at all about "that job."

The rest of April ticked along as normal, but in May the minutes seemed to crawl along dragging the days behind them. Wasn't it time for Honey to start — how had she put it? — making it hard for me *not* to see her?

My mother grew stronger every day, and I went on knocking out favorites over at the Crescendo. The manager even upped my pay. So it's not as if life wasn't carrying on. But I couldn't stop thinking about that Eldorado charging down the highway in the wrong direction in T-minus three, two, one. Some nights, on my way home from the casino, I swung the Chevy around and drove toward Torrent, thinking to check things out. But check what out, and where? Honey knew where I lived, while I didn't have a clue about her. So when the city lights came into view I filled up the tank at one of those lonesome, floodlit stations on the outskirts, turned around, and headed back to Buckthorn. One night I thought I saw her pass me going the other direction, so I wheeled the Chevy around and set out in pursuit, and by the time I caught up with her I was back at the gas station again. But of course it wasn't her at all, just some other sleepless woman charging down the highway at 3 a.m. in pursuit of a ghost she couldn't catch.

We were almost into June when the house phone rang one night at about 10, just after my mother had gone to bed. As soon as I picked up she jumped right in with a comment about how she could barely remember her own whereabouts, but she never forgot the number of the old landline we gabbed away on as kids.

We talked for roughly twenty minutes about this and that, as if no time at all had gone by since the drive up to Crystal Lake. She was still in the rented room and on the lookout for work in Torrent. Several job applications were on the go. Pounding the pavement, that kind of thing. She'd heard through the grapevine that my mother was on the mend and apologized for not calling sooner. She had convinced herself that I knew her number and that I'd call if something was up, but then wasn't so sure after all and decided to risk being pushy.

"So here I am. And I want to catch up with you, find out how things are going. But in person, if that's okay with you. Would you meet me? For dinner, I mean?"

I didn't say anything for several seconds, and I don't know why, since I'd known the answer before the phone rang, days before. You know that old saying: she knows the words but not the music? Well, I knew the words *and* the music but, for some reason, couldn't get down to singing — until she said, "I know how much you've got on your plate and I've come back dragging a fair bit of crap with me. Just tell me you're taking care of yourself, and let me know if I can do anything. You can always call me back, if you want, when things calm down. Dinner, or lunch, anytime you say."

I put the pause behind me and fell right in.

And I didn't think about those few stuck seconds again, at least not until much later.

4.

I SETTLED IN AT A TABLE next to the front windows so I could keep an eye on the parking lot and, you know, get a jump on her arrival. I hadn't been to Chez Antoine for years, not since it was Café Stella and Honey and I had once, at fifteen, had a mind-blowing, budget-decimating lunch with Inez.

Nobody admitted the occasion was to celebrate the old man having left home never to return (by June they thought he was gone for good), but that's what it was. And that explained why, for the first and last time, money was no object. Inez simply burned through a personal credit card she'd found in the zipped compart-ment of his abandoned golf bag. "He hid the card with his balls," Honey said, which caused quite a bit of hilarity by the time the three of us had started in on the Chardonnay.

Inez wore her favorite saucer-sized sunglasses and a leather fedora with a feather stuck in its brim. Honey said the hat made her look like a pimp, or a pimp's wife.

"I hope you never have cause to know what a real pimp looks like," Inez told her, as she lit her Player's Light. When the waiter hustled over and asked her to put it out she asked him what his problem was, because after all we were seated on the patio with all sorts of fresh air wafting about.

I would have been embarrassed if my mother had done this sort of thing (and it would have meant she really had lost her mind) but Inez had the rock-star moxie to carry it off, and because we were with her we were a rock star's kids.

I'd never had a drink before that lunch with Honey and her mother, unless draining the last inch of my father's beer at age eight, while he watched the ballgame, could be counted as a drink. Honey, on the other hand, had been kicked out of junior prom for being drunk, or high, and making out with some boy on the dance floor, which was an exaggeration, because I was there and she'd barely touched the guy. She just made it seem as if she had. Still, the three of us made so many toasts that day, and Inez gave us "just a splash" of so much Chardonnay that soon I was too dizzy to think. Add to this the variety of specialties she ordered: calamari, garlic bread, two kinds of pasta, mini pizzas, a plate of greens, cheese, fruit, dessert. And more splashes.

Stella's was intimate, the patio tiny. Some of the diners found us annoying even before Inez lit another cigarette to "round off the banquet" and refused to put it out. The manager insisted we leave and I was just remembering all of this (and barfing in the back seat on the way home) when I saw Honey pull into the lot.

Dust swirled around the Eldorado as she came in off the highway and up the side road to the parking lot, more like coming in for a landing. She got out and shoved the door shut with her hip.

She had one of those tiny leather purses, not much more than a wallet with a long strap, and she tucked it between her knees while she pulled a sweater over her head. I figured she had left the key in the ignition as she'd done since the old days. She always said the car was so temperamental nobody would figure out how to get it started, never mind drive it away. I watched her bunch her hair, or some of it, into an elastic as she crossed the parking lot, the tiny purse bouncing on her hip, the cuffs of her jeans half lodged in her boots like some kind of buccaneer. There had always been, since childhood, so many mismatched clothes, stuff from the thrift store, hand-me-downs from the boys next door. But on Honey everything seemed to add up.

She pushed through the restaurant door, her boots soft on the carpet, dropped the purse on the window ledge, sat down across from me, and leaned in.

"What do you think? Anybody here who might recognize us from the bad old, good old days?" She promised not to order even one item from the celebratory luncheon fiasco, particularly not "that nasty creature in the shell," though we did order a bottle of wine, red, which I'd been getting used to, as I said, while staying with my mother. But "getting used to" isn't anything like savoring. This fact is so obvious, but I'm embarrassed to say that at the ripe old age of twenty-four I had no sense of palate, or any idea, until that night at Chez Antoine, what it meant to savor anything other than a few single moments with my fingertips resting on the keys of a piano. Because what a bottle of wine it was, so red it was almost black. It opened something up in me. The first sip went straight to my head, or somewhere I didn't know, and it carried on from there.

Honey sniffed her glass, sipped, rolled it around. Her theatrical side had returned full force. "Cherries dipped in chocolate," she said, "straight off the vine. And a hint of sun-baked, cracked leather; the kind you find in an old Fiat parked in the sun. Now close your eyes, Nic, and imagine we've pulled off the road next to a sunny vineyard for a little picnic: a stick of crusty bread, a hunk of fantastic cheese. And what else? Let's see: those jumbo olives stuffed with goat cheese, or hot peppers. And fresh butter cooled in a little stone pot of some kind. And, oh, no knives," she said. "We'll tear everything apart with our hands, like the beautiful savages we are." A bit of silence then, while we savored that whole imaginary feast of hers. And I didn't realize how far we'd traveled together until her glass chimed against mine. The wine went down easy, let me tell you.

All through dinner I yammered on. I bored her to death, I'm sure. On and on about stuff she already knew. The gory details of Buckthorn's downhill slide since the market crash, the grand old houses (fire-traps, according to some) broken up into suites, the garbage pit full of crap from Torrent, the wind turbines screwing with people's minds, the sour gas wells, the stalled building developments. Nothing horrible seemed to have escaped my attention since she'd been gone. I felt jolly as I related it all though, because of the red and her.

"Did you know," I whispered, elbow on table, glass tipped toward her, hunched in as if we might get kicked out all over again if someone heard what I was about to confide, "that *all* the apple orchards, and I do mean *all* . . ."

"*All*," she said. "You mean every last one of them . . ."

"That's exactly what I mean. *Each and every one* has been dug up, ripped right out" — you would have thought they'd been ripped, tree after tree, straight from my heart — "and replaced with vineyards."

She glanced at my goblet. "To make wine, you mean?"

I rushed to agree (before I got her point) and then, pretty inebriated, I confessed to being an idiot and said that I'd always been a bit suspicious of fruit-tree huggers anyway. "After all, what's a piece of apple pie in comparison to this fantastic ruby potion sent from the gods," I said, and to hell with how stupid it sounded, because she found it funny, and what else mattered?

My god, life was good that night sitting across from her with all those glasses of wine and laughs between us, most of life's chaos left behind. I mean, life sucked in Buckthorn, but you just never knew what might be waiting around the bend.

And then I inquired about Inez. I told Honey that I couldn't wait to see my mother's face when she found out that the girls from you-know-where were back in the neighborhood, and that she'd be thrilled and relieved to see them again — if things worked out that way.

Honey put her fork down, her plate not yet empty. I waited, eager as ever, to get the scoop. What did I imagine? She'd mentioned they traveled a lot, and how it had taken longer and longer to settle in, so I pictured them screaming down the blacktop in the Eldorado, a new adventure every day. It was dizzying what the two of them could pack into a lunch, after all, or even breakfast. In those early years when I dropped by in the morning to pick up Honey for school, I'd stand in the foyer and feel like I was teetering on the edge of one of those Bruegel prints in my mother's office. A mere three people (before the old man left) seemed to be everywhere at once and doing god knows what. Coffee boiling over. Lost socks. That horrible father hollering in the background while Inez ironed away and dropped cigarette ash onto his pants and the dog chased its bowl around the kitchen. I can still see Honey, wearing the shortest skirt she could find, doing up her blouse as she opened a can of dog food. And the music: full volume at 8 in the morning. Once or twice the cops dropped by to say the neighbors didn't appreciate being dragged into a rock concert so early in the day, which I'm sure left Inez mystified. I was a nervous wreck, late for school every day.

But the point is I pictured them gliding through those lost years like a mother and daughter Thelma and Louise — but a different car, with a different ending. And when Inez got one of her terrible headaches Honey would bed her down in the back seat and carry on through the desert night, her scarf blowing in the breeze, the moon on high.

And it was as if she read my mind because she squared her cutlery up neat against her plate, sat back in her chair, and said, "Shit, Nic. I don't know how to tell you this, so I'll just come right out with it: Inez didn't make it."

I lost my words again — returned to form, I guess you could say. She didn't need to tell me twice. Even then I wasn't one of those people who just can't believe horrible news when they hear it. Instead I thought, *That's how I should have told my mother about my father*, rather than beat around the bush as if somehow I could change the bottom line: *Dad didn't make it.*

Now Inez too. And that's how it goes: people die. One after the next and no letting up, and then it's on to Club Silencio, as Honey used to say after we watched *Mulholland Drive* twice in one night, pulling out all the stops just trying to understand. Because there's nothing that can't be understood if you go over it enough times, right? If you damn well insist on getting the point, and don't let up until you do, all will be revealed.

And for some reason, I guess because my brain was stained with all that magic Cabernet, I heard the echo of Honey's voice say, *Dude's dead, I presume?* And I started laughing and then, you know the old cliché, crying. And Honey had to throw some crumpled-up cash on the table, pull my jacket around my shoulders, and drag me out of there before we both got kicked out again, like back in the bad old, good old days. Or whatever the hell they were.

She drove me around while I sobered up, the windows rolled all the way down and our hair blowing every which way, a reversal of the roles we played as teens when I did the driving before dropping her, still pretty stoned, at home. Since then she seemed to have learned how to handle alcohol, because I would have sworn she'd matched me glass for glass that night and yet never once inched over the double line. We headed back to the lot at Antoine's and I picked up my car. She insisted on following me to the outskirts of Buckthorn before heading back up the highway to Torrent. It was close to 9 by then, but she reminded me how much she loved driving at night, so don't think twice.

We exchanged cell numbers and said goodbye at the filling station where she pumped $10.50 into the Caddy's tank. I wanted to add more, but I knew she wouldn't let me. She reached out the window and took my hand before heading out.

"Back in touch soon," she said. "And we'll have a good long talk about everything."

I watched her drive away, her and the Eldorado bathed in that peculiar light that pours itself down from gas stations at night, and then a flash of red as she tapped the brakes and pulled out onto the highway.

About a week later a guy from Buckthorn Realty dropped by while my mother was at a physiotherapy appointment. He'd called a couple of times and I'd put him off. I didn't want to hear him go on and on about how sorry he was about my father while his eyes measured up the square footage over my mother's shoulder.

The visit lasted about twenty minutes as we stood in the backyard under one of the old maples. He talked about a new development "up the way" and pointed across the highway toward the acres of cornfields rustling in the breeze. I told him straight-away that my mother had no plans to sell. Somewhere along the way he realized we'd taken algebra together in high school so we proceeded to shoot the breeze a little. He never expected to end up selling Buckthorn for a living, or imagined that anyone would want to buy it; I couldn't believe I was still playing oldies and pop standards at the casino, and people wanted to listen.

And then he remarked that he thought he saw Honey Ramone in town the other day, as if the statement was an afterthought. When I didn't reply he added that he'd heard a rumor about "something heavy going down out west." I could see he was waiting for confirmation, so I let out a phoney laugh and said something to the effect that rumors had swarmed Honey like blackflies since she was fourteen, so the chances of "something heavy" being b.s. were sky high, almost guaranteed. Then I looked at my phone, told him it was time to pick up my mother, and we both turned to go.

Something heavy went down out west? News to me. But I'd fall down dead before I dug for more information from a guy from Buckthorn Realty. And anyway, whatever tales he'd heard, they were the usual gnats and rumors. Sure, she made it easy sometimes, but it was all crap in the end.

If there was anything more to say, I imagined she'd do the telling herself.

5.

I TRIED CONTACTING HER a few times (eleven) over the next week. When I didn't reach her I worried that my drunken reaction to the news of her mother dying might have led her to believe I couldn't handle the heavy stuff, what with my own father's death so recent.

Then she called during one of those brief moments when I was thinking of something else. She was at Robinson's clothing store on 3rd, five blocks away, and could I come down and give her a hand with something? I thought maybe the car had broken down as she was passing through on her way to . . . somewhere, anywhere, else.

When I got to Robinson's, the clerk, Lisa Robinson, an old high school acquaintance whose family owned the store, stood chatting Honey up next to the discount blouses. Honey shot a wide-eyed "save me" past Lisa's shoulder as I came through the door. The three of us chatted a bit, and then Honey asked if I'd join her in the change room to offer my opinion on a couple of possibles. Once inside, she thanked me for the rescue and said something to the effect that Ms. R certainly had a lot to talk about for someone who lived in a town where not a fucking thing ever happened.

"I don't think she's gonna let me out of here without buying one of these babies," she said, and nodded toward a couple of blouses hanging next to the bench. She insisted she really did want my opinion, as always, so I sat down while she stripped off her T-shirt. She tried on the pink blouse, and then the white, as if nothing was strange, as if her trying things on in that stuffy change room of our youth, in a department store that was going downhill so fast it had four racks of clothes left, was the most natural thing in the world.

I hadn't realized how thin she was, her jeans low on her hips and belt cinched to the last notch. Even her wrists seemed slight somehow, an elastic band around one of them. Some of her bra's fancy lace had worn away and a tiny brass safety pin held one of the straps together. When she caught my glance in the mirror I got self-conscious about having seen so much and rushed ahead with my opinion: white was the right choice, classic, without a doubt the nicest shirt in the store and it went great with her hair (whatever that meant). And then I felt faint, or what I assume people mean by faint, because it hadn't happened to me before: cold sweat, dizzy, a bit nauseous. She had just tied back her hair with the elastic from her wrist, and I guess she saw my distress and asked if I was okay. I said the room was even stuffier than I remembered, unbearable, and excused myself.

I swept past Lisa at the cash, dodged a bit of Buckthorn Saturday traffic, and sat down on a bench next to the cenotaph. A warm breeze rushed high in the horse chestnuts and down along the footpath in the park. It dried the sweat on my face but didn't seem to cool me. I felt a bit fevered, as if I might be catching a summer cold. For the first time since my father died I recognized how empty I felt and at the same time full of loss. You would have thought one feeling would have displaced the other but instead they ganged up, and I had to lean over with my hands on my knees to get a grip.

Ten minutes later the little bell over Robinson's door rang and Honey came out wearing the white shirt and a pair of beige pants, the old, frayed T-shirt and jeans nowhere to be seen. She came straight over. I figured she'd take one look at my eyes and grill me until I told her what the hell was wrong, and what could I say? The back of your neck is so pale? Your torn fingernails on the buttons of that shirt undid me?

She sat down and rested her hand on my knee, the little plastic price tag thing still attached to her cuff. I took her wrist and tugged it free.

"What a fucking situation," she said. I nodded even though I didn't know exactly what she meant. The comment just seemed a general sort of truth, something you could say anytime at all, and who could disagree?

She slipped a pen out of her purse, searched in vain for a piece of paper, and took my hand and scribbled a street address on my palm. She had an appointment across town at 2, she said, but would I meet her around 7? Then she checked her watch, swore, and rushed back to the car.

I recognized the street address. Anyone within 200 miles would have: Havenhurst, the five-story condo development that had once been the Co-op Flour Mill warehouse north of the county line. The news had been full of stories about its hopes, and failures, back in 2007. People in town said the so-called industrial conversion looked like a big silo and that they should have left the original brick alone instead of spraying it trendy black. But its problems went deeper, especially once the roof started leaking.

People had taken to calling it Haven't-Hurst. All you had to do was cruise by in the evening to see why: the building itself almost invisible in the dark with only two or three apartment windows glowing faintly against the night sky.

It was only a forty-five-minute drive to Havenhurst, but I got there early and cruised around the neighborhood. Not that "the neighborhood" was much more than secondary and gravel roads bordering leased wheat fields and the ghost of the abandoned golf course already overwhelmed by thistle and a sea of long, mauve grasses gone back to nature.

She buzzed me up at 7 sharp, and right away I saw that whatever appointment she'd had that afternoon must have gone well because she was feeling good — and a little stoned. She was always so energetic, even wired, but pot softened and slowed her down to the point of blurriness, but maybe the problem was my eyes.

She wore the same shirt and pants she'd bought at Robinson's, the pants folded up to her knees, the shirt half-unbuttoned in the heat and shirt-tails hanging out. I figured the apartment must be hers, and god knows I looked forward to the tale that led her there, but the surroundings gave nothing away. It could have been anyone's stuff, what little there was — and that turned out to be true. It was a half-furnished penthouse that rented cheap at $950 a month, utilities and parking included because nobody wanted to live at the address, she told me, except a long-haul trucker and a guy who worked the highways twenty miles north, both on the ground floor and hardly ever home.

I was barely inside before she dragged me out to the balcony to admire the view. I'm not good with (or accustomed to) heights so I held back a little, not that it wasn't impressive even for our humble neck of the woods: the shimmering wheat fields stretching off to the east, Fortune Bay in the north, and those deep lakes farther out — a layering of worn mountains to the west. But who really cared about the view just then? I wanted to know what the hell was going on. She sat us down on the sofa and filled me in.

The appointment had been at the bank in Buckthorn. A loan, I thought. But no, they hired her. She started Monday. I took the fact that she was so thrilled about this to be a sign of how low she'd sunk, because the last thing I ever thought Honey would do is work in the financial world, never mind gush about a job at the branch in Buckthorn.

She must have got up and poured me a glass of wine, because there it was in my hand. I couldn't deny that I felt the need for one of those good, long drinks I took while standing alone in the kitchen listening to my mother arrange her wooden tiles into V-I-C-T-O-R-Y.

She told me I looked "a bit twitchy" about her news. I denied it, which wasn't too hard because I couldn't help being relieved about her return. I could hardly believe it. Honey in Buckthorn rather than, I don't know, staring out at the water on some island to hell and gone in the Tyrrhenian Sea.

"It's just I never thought of you as a bean counter, or whatever," I said and then kicked myself for demeaning the very job she'd just managed to find.

"No shit," she said. "But, it pays better than wearing a blue vest with *How May I Help You?* scrawled on the back. At least at the freakin' bank it's a breeze: I take people's money and give it to someone else. At Walmart I'd go off my rocker and bludgeon some asshole with a portable barbecue and end up in the big house, or some nice little domestic cage near my loser hometown."

And here was something new: she said that she'd "done a stint" at a bank in Torrent sometime after she and Inez left Buckthorn. "I had a hotshot job," she said. "Lots of money, for a while. The car, the clothes. But I'm not bragging. I didn't mention it before because now I don't give a shit. I'll spare you further appalling details." I felt awful, like I'd put a damper on her finding decent employment, and maybe that made her pretend to undervalue it. I told her so and apologized.

A tiny ashtray sat on the table beside her, I guess you'd call it a travel ashtray, a little brass thing with a mother of pearl lid. A book of matches lay beside it. She stretched her legs toward me (as we'd sat across from each other a thousand times in the past) and lit what I guess was the rest of the joint she started before I got there. She told me not to feel bad. She knew the job was crap. But it was something to do on the way to something else. She squinted through one eye and offered me the joint. When I held up my empty glass, a reminder that I'd just had a glass of wine she smiled a soft, slow smile and asked if I believed it was possible for a person to feel too good, which, coming from an Italian background, rather than Scottish, I suppose she thought was a rhetorical question.

"Oh, come on. We're not kids anymore. Live a little. I promise I won't let anything bad happen to you," she said and handed it to me. I took the smallest puff, and then another, as suggested, and ever so gradually felt my brain escape my skull and hover two or three feet above. My pupils grew to the size of dinner plates — I was sure of it.

I don't know how long we sat there, silent, like two people studying across from each other in the library at night, lost in our own thoughts I guess. Entirely at ease saying nothing. But I guess that's the point: relax, lose track of time, even though in my racket timing is everything. Through the open balcony door a set of wind chimes — flat silver seashells, transparent and paper thin — stirred in the breeze. Not a sound down in the street since we were a few miles past the outskirts, far away from anything.

At some point Honey asked me what time it was, but vaguely, because it's not like it mattered. I told her it was 10 or so and lapsed back into my reverie. Did a bit more time go by? I'm not sure. I only remember her voice, as if it came from somewhere far across those fields of waving grasses and deep, cold lakes spread out far below her apartment windows.

"I should tell you about my mother," she said.

As she began speaking the evening took on a slow, liquid quality, as if we were lying in a drifting gondola together. Somewhere in the back of my mind I noticed how dark the room had become, but there was no lamp, at least not handy.

So we continued on together through the shadows.

After they fled Buckthorn Honey and Inez drove west. The all-night drives she had described became standard. With nothing to anchor them, the passing of time became meaningless over the days, weeks, months. Dawn, dusk, and all the disorienting miles in between — that was all they knew. It wasn't anything like my romantic view of them: the moon, the scarves blowing in the breeze. Instead, they crashed at motels, the kind with '60s wallpaper and framed prints of ducks flying over marshes. Hot plates. Odd jobs. Gas shortages. Never enough cash.

"Let's just say we rung the hell out those herbal teabags my mother was so hot for," she said. Inez's migraines got worse with the stress of living rough, so Honey took whatever jobs came up in order to pay for living quarters and groceries.

"I was a hideous waitress, and the small towns had hardly any office work. Factory work, what's left of it, burned me out in six months. My best job was doing kitchen prep at a motor lodge somewhere in — oh hell, I can't remember. All I recall is the neon sign on the roof of the motel next door flashing away in the night: Delightful Shores, or rather hores, you know, with the all-important S burnt out. What a difference a letter makes, eh Nic? But we know that from that pathetic game of ours.

"Anyway, I seemed to be something of a natural in the kitchen. I ended up getting two more jobs but sooner or later the chef would want to teach me all he knew, if you get my gist. Or the pot washer started giving me those long eyes and then finally hit on me. Eventually I might go ahead and compromise myself in some way with a customer of a certain type" — she rubbed her fingers together to imply cash — "and pretty soon Inez and me had to set off in the Eldorado again."

The medication for her mother's headaches cost $25 a pop, so behind Honey's back Inez turned to painkillers bought cheap online. One night she disappeared and Honey found her at the bus station counting out her change.

"If there's a more soul-trashing sight than an aging woman digging coins out of her change purse in front of a cashier I don't know what that is," she said. "She decided she was a burden to me. I told her of course she was, and I was her burden too. We were each other's big, fucking pile of trouble to carry, and lift, and drag along with both hands, if that's what it took."

She didn't realize that her mother was losing herself to chronic depression and anxiety. Honey said that if she had known this, she would have made different choices after they moved back to the Noblesse Oblige trailer park (Inez called it the Big N.O.) east of Torrent.

She fell silent then and returned to earth for a moment.

"You're cold," she said and got up. She came back with the comforter from her bed and settled it over the two of us, her legs once again stretched alongside me. One of her feet lay exposed, barely discernible in the shadows, yet how could I see the pale tan lines from the straps of her sandals? Was that a vision from years ago, or right then, that night? It hardly mattered. It's just that I wanted to rest my hand there, as I would've done without thinking somewhere back in time.

"We were two days away from getting tossed out of that pile of crap. Work went downhill because I couldn't let her out of my sight. So when I decided to try for a bank loan she had to tag along. I've learned that there's a definite craft required in getting a loan from someone — man, woman, or child. Not that I'd ever knock over a kid's Kool-Aid stand, or anything." She stretched, yawned, and tossed her side of the comforter away.

"I spent a fair bit of time getting dressed that morning, if you know what I mean, and fingers crossed the financial associate would be a guy. Don't get me wrong, I'm no slouch with women either, but it's a whole different hustle. You need to be deft with women, a lighter touch. You know — use your words and take your time. But get in and get out before she begins to feel remorse about surrendering something she'll regret later. Not regret, but think twice about. A loan, I mean. Fortunately she'll deny it happened, even to herself never mind the bank, so nothing will be rescinded. But *use my words*? I could barely put two words together, and we didn't have a lot of time." She paused and lit another joint, offered it to me. I watched my fingertips accept it, raise it to my lips, then sat up, coughed a few times, and handed it back. She put it out and placed it in the tiny ashtray, leaned back, her arms beneath her head, and gazed at the shadows flickering across the walls and ceiling in the moonlight.

As it turned out, the manager himself ushered the two of them into his office and closed the door. Honey gave him the once-over and decided the loan would be "like taking candy from a baby with a bad goatee," because the guy couldn't take his eyes off her. "So rude and gross. And right in front of my mother!" She laughed as she told me, because she remembered that his predictable response was exactly the kind of distraction she intended, expected, and could always rely on. "Money in the bank," she said. "Just not *his* bank."

She had told Inez that the chances for a juicy steak and glass of overpriced Shiraz that evening would be increased if she let her do the talking. When Inez complained about being reduced to a prop Honey said, "That's right: you're the dignified, silent fucking matriarch prop, and you have to play your part to a tee or stay in the car."

She pulled the blanket over herself again and lay back. "I felt like shit talking to her that way because she was far from full strength, but my own nerves were shot too."

Inez had dressed for the occasion as well: fancy scarves and silver bangles and all topped off with the ever-present handbag, a Coach hobo Honey claimed she ordered special from Saks Fifth Avenue, a good joke because they both knew it was a fake she'd bought on a street corner from someone as desperate as they were.

The manager (mid-forties, hefty) fiddled with his computer, the smell of leather and aftershave — "Hugo Boss," Honey said and pretended to gag — wafting around him while she laid out the situation, minus the desperation. Maybe if Inez hadn't come along she would have been more transparent, among other things, she said. Her mother had lost a lot but not her dignity, so Honey told the manager they'd been traveling for a few years but now felt the need to settle down. She hoped that "traveling" would imply something like kicking back in Thailand or hiking in Nepal — but she knew the guy didn't buy it. "I mean, all the poor slobs he turned away in a day? He knew as soon as he laid eyes on us." Even so, she played her part and put her trust in the "hot quotient." She told the manager their requirements were straightforward: a simple loan to get them back on their feet. Say, $5,000.

He asked for an address. Honey said a lease was in the offing, only a matter of time. He inquired about employment. Honey said she'd never had a problem securing a job.

"Never?" he said. "Even in this climate?" Honey didn't like his manner. "You know the type, Nic," she said and pulled her ear. "Little gold stud. And that suit. Those shoes. The bald guy buzz-cut."

When he made the climate remark Inez said she didn't see what the weather had to do with anything. Honey ignored this, but the manager was amused, even delighted. He laughed and apologized for confusing things. "Of course I meant the financial climate, Mrs. Ramone." Now and then he sent a conspiratorial glance Honey's way. She refused to return it.

"Well, ladies," he said. "I'd like to help, but you're making it a bit tough for me here. Do you have anything of value, any collateral at all?" Before Honey could answer Inez said, "We sure do. We've got a knockout vintage Cadillac. Never driven outside Texas until we bought it with 20,000 original miles. Leather upholstery. And it wasn't cheap, let me tell you."

"Is that the car you're talking about?" he said and tweaked the louvered blinds. All three looked out at the beat-up Eldorado parked at the far end of the lot, alone, as if no other self-respecting car would be caught dead next to it. Honey said that would have been a good time for the license plate to fall off, and she couldn't believe it didn't, the way their luck was going.

He sat back. "Look, I'm sorry," he said. "I really am. Because I know how challenging things are right now. But I just don't see how the branch can help you. Maybe come back after employment is secured and you've got a residential address nailed down and per- haps we can figure out some sort of modest loan." He gave Honey his card. "Please do call," he said and looked her hard in the eye.

She had just begun processing the look, weighing the idea of securing the loan in some other way — a speedy transaction (she was sure of it) with no interest whatsoever — when Inez took a gun (*the* gun) out of her purse and said, "How much could we get with this?"

I thought Honey was putting me on. Or maybe drinking wine and toking had turned me into a character in one of our old thrillers. She admitted that, for a second or two, she felt the same way sitting at the bank that day: the pistol in her mother's hand (her bangles trembling), the bank manager recoiling in his leather swivel. She hadn't figured on her mother digging the thing out of the Corn Flakes and packing it in her purse like some kind of new age Bonnie Parker. Just when she thought it couldn't get any more frantic, Inez cocked the trigger. She expected the guy to hit some kind of alarm, or lunge toward them, or scatter the chairs as he took cover under his desk. In Honey's mind they were already at the police station with a shitstorm of trouble raining down — but instead he got very calm.

"Ms. Ramone," he said, "will you please take that gun from your mother's hand, uncock it — I have a feeling you know how — and put it back in that very nice bag of hers?" Which she did, and then he turned sweet as pie, Honey said. You know, he went on about these being hard times and shit happens and no harm done — along those lines. "You would have thought he soothed away dozens of mother/daughter hold-ups every week," she said. He escorted them to the door and wished them well. Told them to be careful.

At the last minute he drew Honey aside and asked for her phone number so that he could follow up and see how they were making out. She felt obliged to give it to him.

All the way back to the Noblesse Oblige she tore a strip off Inez, demanded to know what the hell had come over her to pull a stunt like that. "You want to get locked up with a bunch of nut jobs, is that it? They'll make fast fucking work of you and all that jangly bling, let me tell you. Don't expect me to row out and visit you in some goddamn old lady's Alcatraz every weekend. I've got my hands full, in case you didn't fucking notice." And on and on, furious and scared. Inez watched the scenery rush by and denied she ever would have shot the man.

"You cocked the trigger!" Honey said. "It sounded like somebody dropped a rusty hammer into a bucket. I'm surprised they didn't hear it at police headquarters, or wherever."

"But it wasn't loaded," Inez replied, impatient.

"Did that prick know as much? Did I? For god's sake, Mother. You could have gotten us killed by some hopped-up security guard. Or what if the fucking banker had a gun too? Jesus."

"Men like him pull hold-ups themselves all day long. They just don't have the balls to use a pistol. Please stop berating me — and pay attention to the road."

"Oh, that's just beautiful: the pistol warning the bullet to be careful."

"It's no good letting the man think you don't have the nerve to use a gun if it's right there in your hand. You have to at least go through the motions," Inez said and then lit a cigarette and went quiet until Honey lurched to a stop outside the mobile home.

"I'm just tired of everything," Inez said and threw the cigarette out the window. "I needed something to happen. Sometimes people just *do* things."

They were still at odds when, three days later, Gold Stud called and offered Honey what he called "an amazing opportunity for advancement." This is when she realized why they didn't get the loan that day. "Turns out it wasn't because I was slipping or something. You know, losing my edge. It's just that he saw the opportunity to get something from me instead. I kind of suspected as much. But you still worry."

She declined the job at first. What did she know about banking? He said he'd teach her everything he knew, which seemed to be a lot according to his business card: Don Aurbuck, CFA, CFP, FRM, and a couple of others she couldn't remember. She only "toppled," as she put it, because she and Inez were so desperate.

"But about my mother," she said, and then went on for a while about how you should tell a person good things as soon as they happen, don't wait for some ideal time in the future. Don't even wait a few days, she said, because that's what she did. After securing the job with the Commerce in Torrent, Aurbuck offered her an advance so she and her mother could settle in somewhere, all on the hush-hush, not a word to Inez. And then she planned the perfect unveiling of their new life.

"I figured I'd take her to the salon first, get her hair done, then out for dinner to stuff her with a nice filet mignon, super-rare, none of that medium-well crap, and maybe matchstick frites and heirloom carrots sprinkled with salt from the Himalayas or some goddamn place, even though all those fancy salts are just bullshit. And never mind the wine, we'd go for a bottle of La Grande Dame, you know, in honor of all the original grand ladies, and a whole cart of fucking to-die-for desserts; and even if she went ahead and dropped a few of those high-end dinner rolls into that knock-off hobo bag at her feet — and she would — I wouldn't say a thing. Because who really gave a shit? So last day at the Noblesse Oblige I came home after signing a lease on a little bungalow thirty-five minutes from Torrent. It had a massive willow, like a big gushing fountain in the backyard, like at the old duplex on Argyle. Remember?"

"Oh yes."

By then it must have been midnight, or later, and the quiet had deepened, the delicate chimes on the balcony almost inaudible in the breeze. The sky was clear, almost shiny, but now and then a patch of cloud drifted over the moon and rippled shadows through the apartment. Honey lay back and gazed up as the little patches of soft light came and went.

She said that Inez just didn't make it as far as her brilliant plan, and that half the time Honey felt like she was stuck in that restaurant waiting for her mother to waltz in, stuff herself, and rip off the dinner rolls. I thought she was on the verge of saying more, but something about her manner, and my blissful sense of timelessness, made me patient, content not to push. She merely added that her mother was right: sometimes people get desperate waiting for something, anything, to happen. And they do something stupid.

6.

SATURDAY, LATE AUGUST: I asked my mother if she felt up to taking a spin in the country, as she and my father had often done on the weekends. We cruised north as far as Dry Creek, had lunch at a tea room in Arnot, and then stopped by the fairgrounds to watch the roustabouts dismantle the Ferris wheel in the last of the summer rains. Ordinarily the grounds stayed open until Labor Day, but Buckthorn's charm couldn't compete with the bigger fall fairs down Torrent way. The whole thing had become a habit, just going through the motions — a big wheel turning with nobody on it. The roller coaster was already down, the teacups from the kids Tilt-A-Whirl tipped over next to them, and the carousel horses with their wild manes and colorful saddles lay on their sides in the grass. We sat there awhile thinking our own thoughts — the ghost of my father between us.

On the way home she suggested we have a look at some of the developments east of town (though she knew there was nothing to see but cracked foundations and rusting rebar) and then we might swing by Havenhurst. I asked why she wanted to see that eyesore. "No reason in particular," she said. "It's just the closest we have to a famous local landmark these days it seems. If you want to head home, that's fine with me."

I still hadn't mentioned the prodigal's return, hadn't been thinking about that aspect of things at all, and it occurred to me that when my mother felt up to doing her personal banking again, rather than having me do it for her, she was bound to run into Honey and wonder why I hadn't said anything. This oversight might renew her tendency to be touchy about Honey and her mother's disappearing act.

So I told her the whole story, everything except the part about the gun and that Inez "didn't make it," as Honey put it. It was a lot of information, and still my sense was that she knew I had left something out. She quizzed me all the way home and into the house, trying to figure out where I'd hidden the weapon, so to speak, the little gun-shaped piece missing from the center of the puzzle. Where did you say they went out west? When did they come back? You're saying that car's still on the road? They were 200 miles south of Buckthorn all these years? I answered each question as best I could and then she went quiet. If there's anything worse than my mother asking a pile of questions, it's her asking them and then suddenly falling silent: the baton comes down and the whole orchestra waits but doesn't relax.

I busied myself doing the things people do when they want to avoid continuing a conversation. Adjust this, fuss with that. I ambled into the kitchen, opened a few cupboards, closed them again. But then habit got the better of me and when I brought her a glass of water she renewed the questioning. Nothing shrill, just her usual reason over passion combined with that sensible tone that was so hard to match. She took a few sips of water, because it's hard work, getting to the point.

"Have you seen a fair bit of Honey since she got back?"

"We've met a couple of times."

"And it all makes sense — what she's told you about these last six years?"

"Sure," I said. "Why not? Just because they had the balls to get out of Buckthorn doesn't mean she's full of shit." A little pause here while we both considered my overreaction to her simple question.

"I understood them leaving Buckthorn, Nicole. I just didn't get them going on the lam without a word — except for that mystifying note left in charge of . . . Mr. Dude."

"You're still mad about the dog."

She gave me one of those long, low looks that meant *don't be an idiot*. "You've forgotten how long it took you to get over that whole thing?"

"They didn't just *run off*, you know. They ran away. From that awful old man. Why are you being so stubborn about this?" There was an inch of water left in her glass. She swirled it around a few times and tossed it back the way some people knock back a belt of scotch to give them more nerve. My mother only required water — straight up.

She set the empty glass on the table. "What happened to Inez?"

"Happened?"

"You said she didn't make it."

Now here was a question you'd expect a straight answer to. Except I didn't know the answer, and how odd would that seem? For a few seconds I couldn't speak as I recalled Honey and I stretched out alongside each other, drinking, toking . . . *I should tell you about my mother . . .*

Finally I said, "I'm not sure about all the details. Honey was a bit distracted when she told me."

"Is she alright?" The way she posed the question (she really wanted to know) was a departure from the style of question and answer we'd been exercising up until then — a Ping-Pong game winding down. I told her that Honey was just getting on her feet, looking for work, nailing down a place to live. We both sat there a bit longer. She picked up her glass and wiped the table underneath with her sleeve. I waited for her, the chairwoman of the board, to adjourn the meeting. But she pushed up her sleeves, so I knew there was another question coming. "Has Honey been in the neighborhood lately?"

"What do you mean?"

"Just what I said. Has she been driving around the area?"

"Was she in the Caddy?"

"No."

"Then it wasn't her." I could see her consider further queries, and then decide against. She got up, picked up her empty glass. "Well," she said, "I'll set the table."

Thank god, freedom at last. But not so fast. As she passed me on the way to the kitchen she rested her hand on my head, like I was ten, something she rarely indulged even when I *was* ten.

"Be careful," she said. "I don't want to see you hurt again."

I made a salad, grilled us a couple of chops. And then I remembered I had a three-hour set to play at the Crescendo in twenty minutes — saved from further pointless discussion by that pointless job of mine. I squeezed myself into my crooner's uniform — the black skirt, white blouse, dollar sign cufflinks — and out I went with half a chop between my teeth and a napkin stuffed in my collar to save the shirt.

I had to laugh at myself because all the way out to the highway I felt disappointed that Honey wasn't stalking me.

I threw in a few extra songs that night, just for fun. It's not like I had anywhere to go in Buckthorn: "Corcovado," "Poor Side of Town," "Don't Explain" — that sort of thing. The regulars never tired of "Poor Side."

When I left the casino sometime after midnight I was wound up, as usual, so I took the long way home: Highway 7 up to the Dry River cut-off, then left at the old barn on County Rd. 8, and back into town past the string of motels, all of them nailed shut except for the Villa Capri, then through town via the main drag.

I'd just turned onto Broad Street and was thinking of topping up the tank at the Co-op when I saw her sitting in a booth by the window at Blink's Diner, an all-nighter that served 24-hour breakfasts and the usual hot beef sandwiches with mashed potatoes and fries, that sort of thing. At that hour the patrons were mostly guys heading up north to blast rock early in the a.m., or truckers with cargo heading south to the city. I pulled over across the street, switched off the ignition, and pushed the door open, thinking to join her. But when I noticed the phone pressed to her ear, I changed my mind.

I don't know why I sat there studying her for so long. At first I thought she'd notice my father's old Chevy and wave me in, but she never looked up. Whoever was on the other end of the line, things didn't seem to be going well. She leaned into the conversation like you do a wind, her fingers shielding her eyes. The last time I'd seen her look that ill at ease she was telling me about her broken arm.

A gray suit jacket lay draped across the back of the booth beside her and she wore a dressy pink shirt. I knew she'd worked Saturday but still, the early 2 o'clock closing at the bank was a long way behind her. The Honey I knew would have been hot to get home, strip off the uniform, and relax in a pair of cut-offs and T-shirt, glass of wine in hand. But where was her car?

A cab sped by, probably on the way to the bus station downtown to pick up a fare or two on the last express from Torrent, and then a police cruiser. How embarrassing would it be if the cops eased up beside me and wondered why I might be sitting in the dark staring at a woman having a private phone conversation at Blink's Diner? When the cruiser disappeared I started up the car and prepared to pull away, but then a van turned the corner at Broad and Oak and I waited for it to pass, along with that low bass heartbeat of a sound system. It slowed in front of Blink's and blocked my view of Honey for what felt like a full minute and then continued on. I adjusted my mirror and watched it make a three-point-turn, drive back up the street, and cruise past again. Then it proceeded up to Broad, turned back onto Oak, and vanished — the thumping bass beat fading away with it. I sat there thinking about vans and their whole suspicious vibe, especially with those tinted windows. You could take them for granted as they bustled here and there all day, but in the later hours the loners stood out; all that room freed up in the back after the day's deliveries. A loop from *The Silence of the Lambs* rolled through my mind: the van, the pit, the woman in the pit. The guy who wanted to steal her flesh.

That did it: I swung the car around and parked a half block down from the café with the motor running. Should I wait or head into the diner? Either way, she was going back to Havenhurst in my father's Chevy.

I still hadn't decided what to do when in the rearview mirror I saw the restaurant door swing open and out she came with the suit jacket over her arm, yanking her skirt down. She paced along so quickly that I hardly had time to back up before she reached me.

"Oh thank god," she said and tossed her jacket in the back. She threw herself in beside me, slipped off her shoes, and dropped them on the floor with her purse. Her phone rang right away from somewhere deep in the folds of her suit jacket. She ignored it. But when it rang again she fished it out, turned it off, and tossed it back. I said something like, "Does somebody need to make an emergency withdrawal from the bank, or something . . ." But I saw her distraction and let it go. She pushed her shirt cuffs up past her elbows and sat with her hands behind her head, half-moon sweat stains under her arms. I had been listening to Billie Holiday, weighing the idea of trying a new number on the casino crowd — say, "Fine and Mellow," or "Summertime," what with the heat wave holding. She reached over as I pulled away from the curb, edged the volume up a notch, then sat back and watched "our good old horrible" pass by, her cheek flickering on and off under the row of streetlights.

When we got to Havenhurst I noticed the Caddy parked in its usual spot. I pulled in beside it, turned off the ignition, and we sat there listening to the music, her bare feet on the dash, head tipped back against the seat. The late hour meant it was early Sunday by then, but at least neither of us had to work that day. She asked how my night went, commented on my cheesy cufflinks, expressed amazement that I could sit down in that skirt, never mind play piano in it.

"That's *all* I can do," I told her. She smiled, ran her hands through her hair, and turned the volume down a notch.

"Well. Will you look at us," she said. "Two hot babes with nowhere to go. How the hell do you even get in trouble in Buckthorn anymore?"

I laughed and suggested we drive around until we ran out of gas, like in the old days, and she said, "That fucking bastard."

Her eyes were on the Eldorado the whole time. I thought maybe the car had broken down after all, and she had to fork out the cash to have the beast (okay, bastard) towed back to Havenhurst. She shook her head as if to say no, that's not it, and whispered, "Scumbag."

She yanked the door handle, got out, and started across the parking lot barefoot. I gathered up her shoes, purse, jacket and followed. Not a word all the way up in the elevator. She let us into the apartment and switched on the overhead light, the same kind of useless designer chandelier that barely lit the lobby. I dropped her stuff on the sofa and followed her down the hall to the bathroom. She left the door open, as usual, hiked up her skirt, sat down.

"What the hell is going on?" I asked.

"I'd tell you, but I'm not sure how much you can take."

"All of it," I said. Naive of me, as it turned out.

Of course I had wondered about the manager at the bank, that Don Aurbuck character, not to mention his tricky employment offer. I figured that's what Honey meant when she referred to a "hotshot" job, nice car, pricy wardrobe.

It turned out she had a lot more going for her than that. She'd just turned twenty-one when her and Inez came in off the road, all those failed attempts to thrive in various small towns and assorted jobs behind them. A year after she accepted the job at the branch in Torrent she was driving Aurbuck's Corvette, his MG, whatever fancy car she wanted (though not to work, he discouraged that — too flashy) and living in his condo next to the Four Seasons downtown. She was a quick study at the bank. Had a head for numbers; after all she'd been the Crescendo's best (under the table) croupier at sixteen. That was fine, but Aurbuck made his real money in online trading and a few other things he had going on the side.

Dinners out every night, parties, holidays in hot places. Summers they drove up to Aurbuck's old family cottage on Silk Lake. Three generations, he told her. Old money. Honey said it looked like a cottage from an old magazine. A mahogany motorboat with a catchy name scrawled on the stern in gold leaf and tethered to a dock with a hot tub at one end and a tiki bar with a grass roof at the other. A caretaker, a local guy from Port Union, the nearest town, lived in a cabin on the property all summer and fall — twenty acres so you never knew he was there until his services were needed. Whenever called upon he'd cast off, gun the massive inboard into a low, churning growl, and cruise guests to the luxurious (yet quaint) marina to buy cigars and wine and special order lobster and steaks for the barbecue, which Honey said was really a massive grill installed in an outdoor kitchen. Everything about Aurbuck implied he came from money and was making more of it.

"He might have had twenty-five years on me, but still he had his charms," Honey said, "if you know what I mean."

Of course I didn't. Was she talking about the boat, the cottage, the trips? Or was it the sex: the things an older, experienced man might teach a beautiful young hick from Buckthorn? I didn't ask for details. I tried not to look as if the only thing "threesome" meant to me was piano, cello, and violin, but she knew me well enough to know better, even with the six lost years figured in. It seemed the combination of money, sex, and drugs led to some wildly unorthodox nights. She said it was fortunate that she was high or stoned a good part of the time and couldn't remember all the sordid details.

Two years into the relationship, just as she began to question why a guy rolling in dough would hang around a ho-hum bank from 8 to 4, even as manager of a main branch in a major city, she found out that his extracurricular activities weren't exactly on the up and up. Pretty soon hers weren't either. She turned out to be quite an asset.

"It's just not that hard," Honey said, "to rip off people's bank accounts, especially retirees — older folks who can't keep track of their prescriptions, never mind their savings and investments. Especially if they have complex portfolios, and maybe a dormant account or two. The position of trust: that's your strong point. Play your cards right, and certain clients will eventually refuse to deal with anyone but you. If you own a top-notch cologne, one fitted cotton dress shirt in, say, buttermilk or biscotti, a tailored suit, two pairs of pearl earrings — one black, one white — and if you back it all up with a pair of heels so elegant they make a certain type of financial guy sick with envy, well — you're halfway there without lifting a finger. More than halfway if you also have personality. But all the rest comes first. Don't look at me that way, Nic. It's not like I'm defending this bullshit way of the world. I know it's not fair. I'm just saying that's the way it is. And sometimes you've got to make the most of the way it fucking is."

She also realized that Aurbuck's interest in her during the meeting she and Inez sat through that first day hadn't been a coincidence. He'd recognized her from a website.

"What kind of website?" I couldn't imagine what it would be. She'd never been big on social media even back in our teen years — too much of what she called "stupid stuff" from guys.

"I don't know how else to say this, so I'll just come out with it." She said that when things were at their worst with Inez she disguised herself as best she could — cut and dyed her hair — and did some online porn to pay bills; six months at most but long enough for Aurbuck to see and remember her.

"You might be surprised to know how many guys get off on a girl who's made herself up to look like a young boy — I mean, except for the obvious — with smoky eyes and wearing a little too much Vamptastic Plum lipstick," she said.

Might be surprised? I'm sure my heated-up face told her how right she was, and I couldn't help wondering, while not really wanting to know, what exactly would be the "right" amount of plum lipstick for a woman who looks like an underage boy to wear? And what on Earth did this whole scenario lead to? And for how long? I sat there despising that Aurbuck pervert — and wondering what he saw.

We were sitting at a table with a cold teapot between us, her cup empty, mine full, now cold too. I felt her eyes taking me in, measuring my response to the news. I found myself thinking fondly of that flask of hers.

"I hope you're not going to get all cardigan sweater on me, Nic," she said. I pretended not to know what she meant. She'd taken my silence as judgment. That wasn't exactly true. I was surprised, sure. But mostly I was angry she hadn't come to me back then, rather than get involved in desperate situations, and told her so.

"We were what — eighteen?" she said. "Your mother was all over you for ignoring your child prodigy when I left. Nobody had any fucking cash. And I was supposed to call you up out of nowhere, literally, and hit you up for a couple of hundred bucks so I wouldn't have to flash my tits online?"

I reminded her that I could have offered support in other ways. "Everything's about money with you," I said and then felt awful, because I knew it wasn't true. The circumstances were rotten, that's all.

"Oh my god, Nic. I've done worse shit than flash my naughty bits, fake a little ecstasy, and talk dirty to a bunch of guys living in their mothers' basements — or, more often, a hotshot rich guy behind closed doors at the bank. The so-called legit crowd in their skinny designer suits and patent loafers? Now, there I've pushed some boundaries. The fucking godawful stories I could tell you."

She gathered up our cups, tossed them in the sink, then turned back and said, "And you're wrong. It's not all about money with me. I'm sorry to have to interrupt the Chopin Étude or whatever you're living in, but I'm not the one who decided that every fucking thing in this world depends on cold, hard cash."

"You probably mean a Bach fugue," I said.

She stared at me for a beat or two. "I'll bet you're right," she said.

She unzipped her skirt, stepped out of it, then disappeared into the bedroom. Over her shoulder she said, "Nevertheless, you've muffled yourself, let's say, from certain aspects of the real world. Are you even listening to that Billie Holiday stuff you like so much? Ask her. She'll tell you."

I ignored that remark and hollered back, a little louder than planned, that I didn't want to hear any of those awful stories she referred to.

"You might not have any choice," she said as she came back, wearing an old T-shirt and shorts. She sat down at the table again, serious then, and sober. She confessed that Aurbuck had been calling her for days, that he wanted her back, but because he knew that was impossible he wanted his loan back instead. She said in his mind the loan comprised all the money he'd spent on her while they were together: the free rent, the clothes, the up-keep on her car, dinners, vacations, and on and on. Everything he could think of.

"He probably wants to be repaid for every tube of toothpaste and box of tampons. As if I didn't *over*pay every single night I spent with him. It amazed me how he could transform on a dime into that loan manager my mother and I dealt with that day at the bank. I almost wish the damn gun had been loaded, then I wouldn't have had to listen to him go on and on about the many ways he'd protect himself and expose me 'for the depraved little slut' I am if I should try to leave him. But then I'm the one who threw away my own conscience, stripped off my clothes, and handed him the evidence."

"He called you what . . . ?"

"I'm sorry for having to talk such embarrassing shit. The man's a triple-decker dirt sandwich, but it's all my own fault. And not for one minute do I expect any sympathy from you, and in fact I would strongly reject it. Because I got myself into this whole jam all on my own, with one stupid compromising decision after the next."

She described how she'd been sitting in Aurbuck's office late one night, one of many, tapping away on the keyboard. This was close to three years into their relationship, both professional and personal, and at the height of the excess of it all — the many insane luxuries she'd spoken of earlier, and more. And yes, sex and drugs had been a big part of everything they did in their leisure time, just as bank fraud (why recoil from the truth at this point, she said) was part of their 8 to 4. She was working late that night, in the very office where she and Inez had sat the day they came in to beg for that loan, before her mother had pointed out they didn't know a thing about begging.

She kept the lights low, just a desk lamp — which Aurbuck had insisted on so as not to draw attention. She said she knew that what she was going to say would sound nuts, but at one point she looked out at the parking lot, empty at that hour, just the cones of light shining down, and there was the Eldorado parked at the far end of the lot. She remembered thinking how fucking good it looked because she'd had some restoration done. It was miles better than the day she and Inez had first brought it home. The memory of that drive over to our place on Montague Street became so vivid it was painful to her, and stark, as though someone had taken a photograph of that moment, drained all the color, and handed it back to her.

"And I'm not gonna claim good old Mom appeared out of nowhere, you know, the fog cleared and there she was in all her unique, let's say, splendor: the thrift-store scarves and crazy hair. It's more that I *felt* her, you know, inside me. And her presence was so real I could hear all those damn bracelets jangling away. It didn't take much to imagine her sitting there, blown away to find me on the other side of that manager's desk fiddling with his computer. I felt her eyes pass over every inch of me, Nic. Her daughter all tricked out in a pink ruffled blouse — did you know you can pay well over a thousand bucks for a fucking shirt? — the gold watch, the boots, the designer jeans . . . the line of coke I'd just inhaled. And when she asked what the hell I was doing I said, 'Well, Mother, I'm just now smack-dab in the middle of moving several hundred bucks out of some retiree's trust account into another trickier account. And then I'll do the same thing three or four more times, call it a night, instead of larceny, and go back to the fancy condo Gold Stud owns. You remember Hugo Boss? And then I'll fulfill a few of his disgusting fantasies so that I can keep the ball rolling and never, ever have to go back to the Noblesse Oblige trailer park where *you* —'" she stopped, as if a sheet of glass had descended between us, and stared into my eyes, searching for some alternative to what she was about to say. But there wasn't one.

"Where you shot yourself with that peace of crap pistol two

days before I would have moved you into the sweetest overpriced bungalow in three hundred miles."

She broke down then — we both did — like she had that last night at Aurbuck's office. That's when she backed out on him, didn't even return to the fancy condo downtown for her things. Just walked across the parking lot, threw herself into the Eldorado, and started driving again.

"And all along the highway, mile after mile, I kept thinking about what a jerk I'd been and all the crap things I'd done and could never make right again. And how easy it was to be that way, you know, based on circumstance and your own crappy weaknesses. That's the scary thing. I'd let this asshole into my world, and I'd joined him in his. But anyway, I drove all night and slept during the day, and I think it wasn't until I crashed somewhere out west, some motel near the foothills with a mother of a T-Rex in the parking lot, that I started worrying about all the terrible shit he had on me, all this stuff I'd colluded in from bank fraud to — well, I'll spare you the gory, but we got pretty wild. And he had records on all of it, one way or another. Yeah, he loved the bullshit girl from the website as much as I came to despise her." She got up, went into the kitchen. I heard a drawer open and she came back with a cigarette. "Do you mind?" she said. "I'll smoke it by the window."

"Sit down," I said. "It's your apartment, after all."

"Yes, but that doesn't mean . . ."

"Sit down for god's sake," I said.

"I shouldn't have told you."

"You're finally home, and then you'd refuse to talk to me? How does that make sense?"

When she tried to light the cigarette her hands shook, so I took it from her, lit it myself, and handed it back to her. "Maybe I'll take up a few bad habits myself," I said.

"Don't do it. They're a bitch to break."

"I mean it. It strikes me that I have shit-all to talk about."

She started to say something, then changed her mind.

"What is it?"

"Nothing," she said.

"There's more, isn't there?"

She drew on the cigarette and flicked it into an ashtray a few times. "It turns out he had a fiancée the whole time we were carrying on. I honestly didn't know about her until later, but who cares? It's not a moral victory because I missed one form of cheating among all the others. And would I have cared if I'd known? There's always a moment, one little beat, when you have the chance to sign on to all the self-serving crap, or say fuck right off. The scary thing is I can't even remember that moment anymore. I'm not sure if those sorts of choices aren't lost to me for good. It's like maybe I've damaged something, corrupted some kind of mechanism in myself, and now it's out of my hands. Do you know what I mean?"

"You're a clock with a broken spring, is that it? Because no, I don't really know what you're talking about."

"Good. Keep not knowing."

"No, I mean I don't think things work that way."

"Well, maybe his fiancée ditched a part of herself too. Because when she found out about me, she lost *something* — that's for sure. And if he'd been able to control himself I might never have known about her. As it was, his need to rage on about what she'd done exceeded his desire for subterfuge, I guess you could say."

"Well?" I'd gone from wanting to hear nothing whatsoever to insisting on hearing it all.

"Alright. Fasten your seatbelt: me and *my man*," here she rolled her eyes and stifled a forced yawn, "headed up to the Silk Lake cottage that last weekend in August. We usually drove up in the Roadster, or the Corvette, but this time he wanted the MG up there too, so he could store it with the boat for the winter. He had two or three cars up there, all fussed over by the guy who took care of 'the estate.' By the way, did you know you can buy a brassiere for a car? I never saw a man more excited to snap on a bra. It took him for*ever*. So anyway, I drove the MG, and he the Roadster, which was fine with me because I loathed getting trapped in a car with him. The man could turn a heavenly stretch of highway into a washboard nightmare. And his taste in music! Jesus. It was like pushing a shopping cart down the aisle of an S&M department store. My head was always pounding by the time we arrived at the cottage, or wherever — so I guess you can't say it wasn't effective. Anyway, about halfway there I caught up with him, hogging the middle lane as always. And I noticed that some of the drivers passing him on the right were slowing and craning their necks. So I eased up beside him. And that's when I saw ... the reason."

"And ... ?"

"*EAT SHIT COP* scrawled on the passenger door's vintage 'banana parfait yellow' paint. So it was pretty striking. He must have missed that little detail in the twilight underground parking at the condo. But how smart of her, when you think of it. Better than *CHEATING PRICK*, or some angry cliché, like a sledge-hammer destroying his windshield. Because of course she knew his weaknesses, where the bodies were buried, so to speak, and how the last thing in the world he wanted was a little chat with the police. I slowed down and dropped right back, as you can imagine. No way I wanted in on that whole scene, but at the same time I just had to see what happened. And sure enough, he got pulled over just before the exit to the lake. He looked like such a jerk, standing there trying to explain why someone would screw with his car. But the best part, Nic? The cop was a woman. And she was mighty freaking impressive, I must say, with that haughty posture and the pistol on her hip. I have to admit I was so delighted I almost had to pull over."

She put out her cigarette. "Can you remind me why we were drinking *tea*? Let's get serious." She got up and fetched two shot glasses and a bottle of that bourbon she liked. "Down the hatch," she said.

"Well? What did you do?" I asked, after I'd tossed it back and caught my breath.

"What do you think? I drove on to the cottage, lit a fire, and went for a nice, long swim."

7.

ANOTHER TWO WEEKS PASSED BEFORE we saw each other again, though we stayed in touch. In fact I called her every other day in case there was news about that prick, which was how I thought of him by then too — him and his little gold stud.

The second week in September we met at the Sugar Bowl on Main for coffee. Wooden barriers blocked the intersections all the way up to Darke Crescent in order to provide safe passage for the Buckthorn charity run. I arrived at the café before Honey, threw my jacket over the bar stool, and watched the racers stretch and warm up in the brisk morning air. The place was jammed with participants and spectators buying hot drinks or a shot of caffeine before the 10 a.m. start.

Not that it was that hard to fill the Sugar Bowl. The place wasn't much bigger than a kids' clubhouse, with four tiny café tables and a short row of stools along the window facing the street, and then the counter with a few pastries on display and the barista behind steaming up the drinks: worn red and cream checkerboard linoleum floor from the days when it used to be an ice-cream shop.

I saw her wending her way through the barricades. I had to laugh because she wore the same navy toque she'd worn the Christmas Eve we walked back to her place after dinner at the house on Montague Street, a Greyhound Bus logo embroidered on the front, one of her mother's thrift-store buys. Just like her to hold on to something like that. Her hair crackled as she yanked it off and sat down beside me. The waitress brought me a latte and Honey an Americano. I asked her how the bank was going.

"I'm appalled to confess that I've impressed the hell out of them with my so-called abilities. The clients adore me. One or two wish to marry me, take me away from all this, shack up somewhere nice."

"You won't be hasty though? Don't take the first shack that comes along."

"Only if said shack is a stone cottage next to a deep, blue sea and a field of lavender blowing in the salty breeze. Oh, and I might as well have a pony and a wine cellar and a nice big kitchen. And my knight in shining armor should turn out to be unexpectedly fragile and then quite quickly dead."

Her manner was breezy, but she looked awful, at least for her: her eyes a bit fevered, that bruised, vulnerable look she got in childhood whenever Inez and the old man were going at it. Her knee beat a nervous rhythm under the table.

"I'm going to lend you the money to cover Aurbuck's loan," I said and tried not to look as surprised as she did, because I couldn't recall anything, any conscious thoughts or plans, that led me to such a decision. I mean, did I wish I could lend her the money? You bet. But actually do it? The offer felt so right that even the bothersome details — that I was broke, for instance, or what the required amount might turn out to be — faded into the background.

She remembered for both of us and politely declined: so sweet of you, can't thank you enough. But no can do. Don't be stupid. She told me that she'd managed to pay back $2,500 since she started working at the bank, had taken out an advance on her credit card to do it.

"Twenty thousand to go," she said, "and I'll be free of the jerk." She said she'd made him promise to return all the stuff he was holding over her head, including personal items, like letters, photographs — every single item that had anything to do with her. "He thinks I can't come up with the money in what he refers to as 'a timely manner.' He's wrong." She added that if it turned out he wasn't wrong, she'd have a big, fat chat with the Eldorado.

Twenty thousand? Jesus, I thought. Still, I insisted on loaning it to her. I can only explain this by saying that the insurance settlement had recently come through and my mother and I had opened a joint account so that I could continue to pay the bills, shop for groceries, and so on. I avoided thinking about this money for the very reason it existed in the first place. Only at that moment did I acknowledge to myself that we weren't exactly "broke" the way we used to be. A fair amount of cash sat in our account, and $20,000 was nothing in comparison. Look at the good it would do in its short absence from the bank.

She resisted, threatened to get up and leave if I kept it up. But who could argue with the wisdom of what I had to say? Because it's not as if this would interfere with my mother's life or my own.

Honey would pay it back, just in a somewhat less "timely manner" than what Aurbuck desired. I still took care of the banking, after all. And my mother was so absorbed in her work she'd never notice, especially since we weren't budgeting to the last dollar anymore.

I pushed on when I saw Honey weaken, urged her to clear the slate with him now, the sooner the better, before he came up with more, or new, terms. That possibility seemed to sober her. I made her promise to call him and nail down a time to make the exchange.

"So, you'll call soon?"

"Yes."

"When?"

"Soon, like you suggested."

"But what does that mean?" Her remark about having to pay him every night lingered in my mind.

"It's just that I can't stand the thought of laying eyes on that asshole again is all."

"Well, how about I do it *for* you?"

"You'll pull on your tough girl trench coat and head on over there to strong-arm the guy? Why didn't I think of that? You're so imposing — all five-foot-one of you. I can just see your sleeves trailing on the ground."

"I'm serious. I can be imposing if I try."

"Right. Nothing more imposing than a small woman in a large trench coat."

"It's all in the eyes."

"You'll stare him into submission. Absolutely not. I'll do it. Because the truth is the guy's more scared of me than I am of him."

"And how does *that* work?"

"I don't know. I'm not talking about holding something over

him, like he does with me," she said. "I've never threatened the guy, in words or attitude — except to tell him to go fuck himself — and maybe something fancier, now and then." She shrugged. "Inez always told me it's the guys who fear you, those are the iffy ones. Don't you just hate that our mothers are starting to be so goddamn right about everything?" She looked me in the eye. "Don't worry. I'll get it done."

I believed her.

Wednesday of the following week she invited me to drop by for a drink.

"Champagne's on tap, and I'm talking the good stuff, not that swill," she said. I went right over, eager to hear the latest installment and certain that I'd never tasted the good stuff.

It turned out she had two bottles of *very* good stuff, and we had just finished the first and were riding high when she finally came out with it.

"Here's to peace of mind," she said and nodded at a box that had caught my eye when I first arrived. It was sitting on the kitchen counter crammed full, I assumed, of all those compromising materials the ex had threatened her with: documents, notes, personal letters, and photographs. Later she told me the photographs were from his artsy black and white collection of "studies": porn that he had matted, framed, and hung on the bedroom wall. As for the rest, she said she had watched Aurbuck delete and wipe clean his laptop of everything she'd been involved in, which seemed practically impossible. So he also signed a document exempting her from personal responsibility or any knowledge of wrongdoing that he wasn't aware of himself when she worked for him. "It's not like it's a legal document. It's bullshit, but at least it's evidence, if necessary," she said. My sense was that she knew it was impossible to make anything truly disappear anymore, especially the rotten stuff. If she wanted to be free of him, she *had* to believe, so I did the same. We toasted again when she showed me the receipt for the money, which wasn't much more than a canceled IOU. Then her face lit up and she began gathering up the second bottle and our jackets.

"Come with me," she said, and down we went in the elevator to her car.

I knew where we were headed as soon as she made the turn at Elm: up to the abandoned campground on Mt. Vista, where bored teenagers went to drink, get stoned, and torch stuff in the moonlight. Not a word all the way up, just an old pop tune or two on the old cassette deck. And no words either as she threw a few dry sticks together and we built a small campfire on the ghost of an old one next to a stand of pines and junipers so fresh you could smell gin on the wind's breath, with twist of lemon thrown in.

She fetched the bottle and box from the car and we sat there getting drunk and, well, torching stuff in the moonlight. When the fire got hot enough she set the box on top and we sat watching it catch and burn while we passed the bottle back and forth; the only sound a series of pops and hisses from the dry wood and the wind stirring the tops of the pines. "Wow, that stuff is as hot as he said it was." She laughed and kicked a few errant pieces back into the flames.

She lit a cigarette. She said she'd quit smoking back at the Oblige but when she started to fret about what Aurbuck might do, that got her going again. There were two left in the package, and after that she'd go clean again.

"But . . . clean again," she said and shook her head. "At what age do people stop being clean, do you think? Eight? Twelve? Twenty? I guess it's different for everyone."

I asked her what she meant by clean, and she laughed, but softly, and said, "Clean is what you are, Nic; otherwise you wouldn't have to ask."

The remark made me feel like a kid. I was getting sick of her innocent take on me. Looting my mother's insurance policy might buy me a few creds, no? I was still searching for something that would make her cringe when she grabbed the front of my shirt, pulled me close, and kissed me. Then she let go.

"There you go. Now you've got a little dirt on you," she said and rubbed soot off my cheek with her thumb. I guess I proved her earlier point, because I didn't know what to say or do — I just laughed.

We sat there a little longer as the fire burned low, the moon a big silver dandelion and all the stars gone to seed around it.

8.

TUESDAY, EARLY EVENING, a couple of weeks into October. I dropped by the florist to pick up something up for my mother, splash a little color around the house now that the garden had been put to bed. I stared at some roses and considered their symbolism. Red for passion, obviously, and the purity (or despair) of white. I wasn't sure about pink but felt certain the connotation would be positive, the blush of modesty, maybe. And then the blue with their whiff of self-delusion.

When the clerk came over I asked her about guilt, the real point behind buying the flowers. She didn't quite get me and said, "What do you want to know?" Then we got on board and she sold me a dozen (cowardly) yellow roses, which I took home to my mother.

When I drove up to the old house Al Carney was laboring away in his yard, all dressed up in goggles and ear protectors and blowing leaves into a corner of the fence with that monstrosity my father had claimed Al had knocked together himself using duct tape, a rusty tailpipe, and the motor from an old Frigidaire. As Fate (and the prevailing winds) would have it, our yard received the lion's share of the waxy horse chestnuts that careened down every fall, while the Carneys were forced to endure two months of leaves the size of dinner plates. He hollered something about them being a bitch to pick up in the rain, and I waved and continued on inside.

My mother was sitting next to the kitchen window drinking coffee and sorting through some papers.

"I'll bet you're relieved we put the plastic on those windows last week," I said as I came down the hall. "I guess you can hear Carney out there blasting his way down the drive with the leaf vaporizer."

I rifled through the cupboards in search of a vase. From the corner of my eye I caught the white envelope and sheaf of papers on the table in front of her. At first she said nothing; the only sound the fading drone of Carney's apparatus and, once I was standing in the kitchen, the faint grind of the electric wall clock, which I had never in twenty-four years noticed before. I put the roses in a vase and set them down on the table in front of her. She glanced at them, and me. "Lovely," she said. A comment like that is fine, on the surface, coming from most people. But my mother's comments didn't always match her face. And here was a case in point, because her lips said what they said, but her face suggested that a few other things weren't lovely at all.

She was wearing my father's old bathrobe, blue with white stripes. She'd been soaking in the tub, probably a long while with Carl Jung or some other smart shrink. Her hair was curly from the steam. I could see the tracks where she'd run her fingers through it a few times; she was never one to stare in the mirror and fuss with her 'do.

I sat down across from her and rearranged the roses, tweaking off a few perfectly healthy leaves, her eyes floating light but firm over my features as if trying to find passage into my thoughts. Her whole demeanor was like someone, chin in hand, scrutinizing a mystifying painting in a gallery with a desire to really *get* what the painter had in mind, rather than a mother looking at a daughter who had pilfered, as far as she could tell, $20,000 out of a tragic insurance payment.

We sat there a long time, it seemed to me, although no more than two stretched-out minutes could have passed before she said, "Does this have anything to do with Honey Ramone?" Jesus Christ, yes, I wanted to say through my hard mouth. Yes, yes, yes. Everything has to do with Honey Ramone. Instead I offered a worse insult: I said nothing.

A pen lay on top of the sheaf of papers and she picked it up, clicked it a few times. I was going to say she kept her poker face, but that's underestimating her. Her aim wasn't to conceal feelings, only keep them in check. How lucky for me, I thought, that she didn't share the sensibilities of Honey's operatic mother or she might have pulled a gun on me.

I had just begun thinking it was a standoff when she dropped the pen, took a deep breath, and said, "You know we're going to have to talk about this, Nicole. So let's get the hell on with it."

So there *was* a bit of an aria in her after all.

"Lovely as those roses are," she said, "I wish you would stop staring them down and tell me what's going on. I take it from your silence that it *is* about Honey. Tell me it isn't also about the two

of you spinning the roulette wheel over at that casino of yours."
And really, how sweet of her, I think now, to assume something so
adolescent and almost innocent in comparison to the truth. But at
the time the point was to avoid, avoid, avoid as long as possible and
give myself time to think, which I was scrambling to do.

"Of *mine*? It's not *my* fault people are over at the Crescendo
throwing their pensions away with both hands. I'm just the pathetic
soundtrack to" — here I dragged out one of my father's old chestnuts, which was unforgivably shitty of me — "*the precariat's misery.*"

We both stared at the roses as if they'd become a painting of
roses — abstract or, if such a painting style existed, obtuse. *Vase of
Roses Caught Between Mother and Thief.* I imagined this could go
on for a while, the two of us being who we were — tight-lipped,
repressed, let's face it. I foresaw the time-lapse roses wilting as they
approached that glorious, frantic, almost dead stage, and the petals
curling and dropping to the table — faded shavings fleeing a sneaky,
hopeless gesture.

"Look," she said, "I don't care about the money. I think you
know me better than that. But I can't have you going behind my
back and doing something like, well . . . *this.* Did you really think
I wouldn't notice? You could have come to me . . ."

"Come to you! Are you kidding? It's not like you're —"

I might as well have slugged her. That was the look on her face,
because she knew that I was about to compare her with Inez. It
took a few beats, more than a few, but she recovered or pretended
to. "That's what you think, that you can't depend on me."

"You *always* thought the Ramones were a mess. Oh sure, you
were polite to them. But you never really took them seriously.
And why? Because Inez threw thrift store scarves over her lamps,

smoked pot, and blasted Bonnie Tyler out the window while Honey cut her hair on the stoop where all the neighbors could see!"

"Oh, for god's sake, Nicole, you don't have to look down on someone to acknowledge that 8 a.m. is a bit early for 'Total Eclipse of the Heart.'"

"I guess you would have been okay with Vivaldi."

"Let's stick to the topic."

"All I know is that the day the two of them came home with that car you could hardly drag yourself out of the potato patch to give it a look. Too flashy, I suppose. Oh, and we owned 'a living room suite' while they were paying installments on a sofa from the Brick with a bunch of crap collecting under the cushions. You never took Inez Ramone seriously because she wasn't like you. She was . . ."

She stayed silent, didn't defend herself even though she knew that everything I accused her of was bullshit meant to distract from the nefarious issue at hand. Inez Ramone didn't take *herself* seriously, that was the answer she could have used and we both knew it.

"Go on," she said.

"She was . . . fun," I said.

She slipped a hanky out of the pocket of my dad's bathrobe. Who else used real hankies anymore, never mind bothered to iron them? She unfolded it, wiped her reading glasses, ready to get down to brass tacks I guess. "Yes, I know she was," she said. "But mothers aren't supposed to be fun."

I didn't say anything to that, but I didn't have to. She looked into my eyes and read what I was thinking, especially since Honey came back: *fun's better*.

She stared at her hands spread out over the tell-tale papers in front of her. And I found myself thinking that if only she'd broken through that therapeutic manner and tore a strip off me, really hauled my ass, I might have laid the whole thing out all in a rush, every detail about Honey, the blackmailing ex, the physical threats, and wound up acknowledging how wrong I'd been. I would have taken the battle on knowing I would lose it, but we'd be straight again, or clean, as Honey put it, and could go on.

Just then the wind gusted and the patio umbrella blew over. Here was my opening, or closing, in a way. I got up, stepped outside to right it, and continued down the steps and around the side of the house to the car.

No answer when I called Honey's cell, so I sat on one of the empty concrete planters at the entranceway and waited. Not one window lit in the whole of Havenhurst that night.

By 9, I'd wandered the parking lot, strolled across the road to the grassy field pulsing with insect cries, took a tour of the abandoned golf course where a few tattered flags still snapped in the breeze, and wandered back to the entranceway again. At least the exercise kept the chill off.

The whole time I debated if I should return to the house and apologize right away or let another hour go by, slip into the house on the quiet, and address the whole mess in the morning. Or should I wait for Honey? But why would I? It's not as if I planned on confiding in her on this particular matter. Why make her feel like shit too? And yet I couldn't seem to get back in the car and drive away. It seemed that I was more desperate than ever for an hour of her banter and a good, stiff drink. I didn't even care what she talked about. I'd just sit and watch her lips move. Where the hell was she?

I had just decided to return to the house when I saw the dust swirl up behind the Caddy and heard the strains of one of Inez's old disco hits. Honey ignored the parking lot, swung around the loop, and lurched to a stop in front of the main door.

Of course she was puzzled at first, because I always called in advance, never did anything unexpected at all, except for that earlier thing. Reliable as a time signature, that was me. She wore a dark wool coat, the collar turned up against her cheek and a scarf that seemed coral beneath the soft light in the foyer. On our way up to the apartment she told me she'd had three martinis and still it hadn't been enough to numb her against the chilling experience of a bank meeting and social event combined. She said she had been forced to prop her elbows on the table to keep from falling asleep and sliding to the floor.

"You know, Nic. I think I may have actually lost consciousness at one point. I remember two or three seconds of relief. But that might have been the gin kicking in. And then — wham — back again. Maybe I've developed that little trick the birds know. Where their claws automatically cling to the twig and keep them upright? My hands agree to hold up my head even while in a stupor."

When we got into the apartment she apologized for bullshitting on and asked if everything was okay. "You look wrung out," she said. I lied and told her all was well, that I just wanted to check in. She changed out of her work clothes and put on some coffee, but when she offered me a glass of wine I told her to bring it on. We sat on the sofa and I helped her fold the laundry into a basket between us. Now and then she took a break to rub her feet while I tried to pace myself with the wine. After we finished folding she dropped the basket on the floor and sat with her coffee cup on her knee, looking at me as if I were an inscrutable object of some sort, turning me this way and that in the half-light.

"Something's going on," she said. When I denied it, she smiled and reminded me how reluctant I'd always been to share my secrets.

"I don't think that's true."

"Oh yes," she said. "Even back in the day you were always a hell of a listener; I just rattled on about every stupid thing. When I think about how I must have bored you out of your skull on the phone late at night with yet another tale about some prick boyfriend . . . but not a peep from you."

"You mean like the one you dumped because he lost his license and you needed a guy with a car?" I said.

"Ouch. I forgot what an unforgiving memory you have." She got up and poured herself a glass of wine. "You were never as heartless as me, never would have used someone and *tossed them aside* when you were through with them. If only I could have been more like you. But we're stuck with ourselves it seems."

"I didn't do any tossing because there was nothing to toss. I pounded away on the Baldwin and hung around with you, and that's it. I had nothing to report that you didn't witness firsthand. No secrets, as I've said. I'm entirely devoid of mystery."

She laughed. "Only someone as wildly enigmatic as you would make such a claim. Everybody has secrets, Nic. That's one thing I've learned at least."

"Well, then you know more than me."

"I don't believe you," she said. I could see her consider carrying on the conversation until she got a rise out of me or until I broke down and told her what was going on. But she let it go.

"I just remembered something," she said and set her glass down. "I found a little something that'll delight both of us, in our own way."

She splashed a few more inches of wine in my glass then disappeared into the bedroom and returned with a box — a piano keyboard inside. She said she found it at the thrift store. "Where else, right? It's probably just a piece of shit. I meant to save it for Christmas," she said, "but as if I could wait." She set it up on the dining room table and plugged it in, a decent little Yamaha. Finding one at a pawn shop would have been lucky, never mind a store full of junk. She pulled two chairs up and told me to get going because she needed a pick-me-up after what the bank had put her through that evening. "And don't be stingy with the crooning either, because I sense in you the need for a little self-expression."

I took another sip of wine, sat down beside her, did that whole theatrical stretching of the fingers thing. Honey laughed and reminded me of that cheesy Charles Aznavour tune that my father would sing for my mother on her birthday every year — the one about maybe she's the beauty or maybe she's the beast, but it really doesn't matter because he'd follow her anywhere . . . and blah blah blah — and how we'd snicker and roll our eyes, right there in front of him. But in spite of my father's overcooked delivery he always got unbearably sincere for the last eight bars, so we'd counter our embarrassment by offering up a bunch of wild, sarcastic applause.

I knocked out a bit of "All of Me" to calm my nerves and take away some of the physical edge. I noodled a bit, a little boogie-woogie, a smattering of ragtime, some "Moonlight Sonata." But when she insisted on a song I surprised myself by returning to the Aznavour tune. At first I hammed it up just like the old man. But then somehow, halfway through I — how can I put it? — the singer's façade broke down, then outright betrayed me, and I did the unthinkable: I got sincere in spite of myself. The distance between me and the lyric closed, the melody took over, took me away. The tips of my fingers seemed to sense every nuance in the keys, even the hairline crack in the bass G. Any hope of going back, goofing my way through, fell away, along with a kind of numbness that I hadn't realized had enveloped me until that moment. I closed my eyes, the only defense I had left, and didn't open them again until the song ended.

In the distance all was dark except for the odd cluster of lights out toward the small towns of Blythe and Travers in the east and then that golden light from the street, worn away to candlelight by the time it reached us from below. I must have known long before the song was over, years before, what was going to happen, that my fingers would move from the keyboard to the front of her shirt, a man's white shirt, but casual, half undone. A pearl on a gold chain rested in that little hollow at the base of her throat, as if it had formed there. We both watched my fingers move from the pearl to the remaining buttons on her shirt as if we were dreaming. But then she woke, pressed her hands against my shoulders, and asked if this was really what I wanted. I tried to begin again, but she made my eyes meet hers. She insisted on hearing my answer because what we were about to do would change everything, she said, and who knew how? But who cared, with her sitting there like that, or sitting any way at all.

This wasn't about words, or intent, or reason — it was the way things were meant to go from the start. Later, I remembered how as children one of our favorite games was to imagine what impossible ability we might give up a year of our lives for: the thrill of being a bird, instead of a dull human? An owl on the hunt? That's how I felt sitting beside her that night, the pearl at her throat, her shirt falling away — and soon, her mouth on mine, the weight of her naked body pressing down on me. She was the impossible thing that, all my life, I was bound to trade myself away for.

9.

I HARDLY RECOGNIZED MYSELF after leaving Honey's bed the next morning, and afternoon, and again in early evening. I stood in her bathroom doing a bit of inventory on that woman in the mirror — whoever she was. The glazed look from lack of sleep (which had never felt so dreamy), the mark on my neck, the agonizing recollection of how she put it there. My mouth looked a bit swollen, it seemed to me, the inside of my lips chafed from her kisses. And those hands, her fingertips, her ... range. It seemed to me that she was the true prodigy. Sexually speaking she could have sat down and played "Rhapsody in Blue" without thinking. Certain other intimacies, when remembered, caused me to avoid my own eyes in the mirror. I had never felt so weak, or more certain that I could accomplish almost anything.

The day after that, I gathered a few wits about me and left my mother a message. When I didn't hear back I dropped by the house. She wasn't there. That wasn't odd; she had taken to walking into town for her last few physical therapy appointments and then having lunch at Blink's. Still, when your own mother doesn't return your calls, you know you're in for it. But I'd planned how I might mend things: put a payment plan together, get another job, and work at paying off the loan myself while Honey paid the loan back to me. And then grovel like hell. Everything suddenly seemed so straightforward, though I wasn't sure about spilling the whole truth about the prodigal and the ex. And what about new . . . developments between Honey and me? My mother might have been ready for that revelation, but that didn't mean I was.

A few more days went by and then, filled with a combination of euphoria and anxiety, I realized it was time to head home and face the music. The weather report warned of an Arctic front moving toward us from the northeast, and on my way back to the house the sky went wide and white, the sun nothing but a candle underneath. I had just pulled into the driveway when the real weather began, snowflakes spinning down and settling on the lawns up and down Montague Street — the sound of a thousand old clocks lost among the leaves.

Once in the house, I dropped my keys on the table and called out. No answer. Honey had given me her sweater and I drew it around me and checked the hall thermostat, inched it up, waited for the furnace to kick in, then continued down the hall. She wasn't in the kitchen, but what did I think — that she'd sat there frozen in time waiting for me to return, take responsibility, wind up the conversation?

No sign of her in the library or the living room. I called out again. No reply. How angry she must be, but who could blame her? I collected a few plates, glasses, napkins, and dropped them in the kitchen sink. The roses sat in the vase next to the banking information. I checked her office, then went upstairs.

The curtains lofted high in the wind over her bedroom window. A crystal vase had fallen from the ledge, its collection of feathers scattered over the rug — owl, raven, and blue jay feathers, mostly, that she had gathered in the backyard over the years. I heard her moan but didn't see her until I came around the bed. She lay on the floor next to her bureau, the comforter half off and twisted around her legs, my father's bathrobe splayed around her. Blood from the gash in her forehead stained the rug next to the dresser. I took her in my arms and tried to unravel the mess, get everything in place again — her in a chair by the bed, the comforter tucked around her. Next I'd bandage her head and make tea, the right way. All would be well. Nothing would be bad. It couldn't be. She was my mother, after all. The whole time I could hear a radio playing distantly, as if it was left under a pillow or something, a voice mumbling away. As I settled her into the chair I caught sight of myself in the bureau mirror and realized the voice was mine. I sounded like a player in one of those overwrought dramas my mother would have suggested I switch off in favor of something "less frantic." I knelt and looked into her eyes, expecting her to say just that. Wishing for it.

And then I called 9-1-1.

After my mother's stroke Honey drove me out to Crystal Lake and back almost every night, just like the old days. We'd sit and stare at the water together, her arm around my shoulder. Sometimes she'd sip from her flask and talk about bank bullshit, just to get my mind off things. On the way home I'd often sink right down and rest my cheek on her knee as she drove, her arm resting on my shoulder, my hand tucked under her thigh. Sometimes I even fell asleep, what with the soft light from the dashboard and a few tunes turned down low. Later I'd think about how I could have died right then, during one of those drives, and been fine with it.

After we got my mother settled into the care home, I dropped by several times each day. I was familiar with the place because I'd played piano for the patients now and then in the years after Honey had left. My mother had recommended it in order to get my mind off things. What would she have suggested I do under the circumstances?

Honey and I discussed how we'd handle things, whatever happened, although there was only so much you could say. Other sorts of illnesses or accidents seemed to lend themselves to involved discussion: Jesus, she fell off the ladder and broke her arm in three places. She'll be in a cast for months. Or, can you imagine the nasty scar after that burn heals? Even a bullet can be dug out and stitched over, depending. But a debilitating stroke and there's nothing to foretell the carnage inside. Everything that existed before seemed gone; her strong gardener's hands at rest in her lap, her unshakeable poise enforced forever.

Some visits I brought Scrabble and set it up between us in her room. I probably entertained some desperate notion that whatever had happened in her brain, her outrageous fanaticism would return, like someone whose hands go on understanding the guitar even though they can't remember their own address. She'd sneak in and seize some sort of victory over that lousy situation after all. But instead it was as if she'd taken a page out of Honey's book and come up with a whole set of new and garbled rules, a kind of incoherent game with no winners. I picked through the letters, spelled out *sorry* on the board, and waited. A sense of dissonance coursed through me, as though the tips of my fingers sought melody and meaning in all the wrong keys.

"Please come back," I demanded. "I'll play this shitty, stupid game with you every day if you do. I'll throw a damn party each time you win. Balloons, clowns, streamers — the whole nine yards." I got up, thinking to bolt the hell out of there. But then I sat back down and held her hand — and when was the last time I'd done something like that, or even touched her at all, aside from the day I found her in the bedroom? "I'm awful, it's true. A rotten daughter. You deserve better. But you know that was all b.s. about preferring Honey's mother over you. You know that was just crap, right?"

I lingered another hour, gathered up the Scrabble game, and kissed her goodbye. Then I drove around to the dumpsters at the rear of the hospital and rattled it into one of them — a final good riddance to that asinine, mind-numbing board game that was only fit for days with so few options that there was nothing in the world to do but sit there shuffling cold, hard vowels.

My mother, the woman I had wanted to escape since I was a teenager, was now with me always. And especially at night, in dreams. I'd wake on some shadowy side road several dreamland miles from daylight, and thank god Honey would be waiting up ahead. She'd pull me into her arms, her lips next to my ear, and draw me in with those recipes of hers as she had at thirteen, fourteen, fifteen while I lay in bed with the phone pressed against my ear. It was like a recitation of some kind or Honey's version of a prayer, if she had believed in such things — her voice lulling me with tales of assorted aromas and things being blended and pounded and how they transform each other after coming into contact with heat. She'd be quiet for a while and then start again with tales of ground pepper, bread soaked in milk, chili peppers, paprika, bitter chocolate, and how a sauce would *liaise* with all sorts of ingredients, without any need of flour, and produce an endless variety of subtle results. I saw the magic of it all. And soon the remorse I felt about my mother would drift out of reach, at least for a while, and my reluctance to sleep was transformed into an inability to stay awake. And then: nothing, which was, at that moment, the equal of yet another form of bliss that Honey had given me.

She died in early November. Honey and I were living together at Havenhurst by then, which was just as well because I couldn't bring myself to go back to Montague Street. I know it's a pathetic cliché to say, but the ghosts, you know? Not that a cliched horror trope was necessary. The bloodstain on my mother's bedroom rug was enough to stop me cold. The vase, those feathers; I could set them back on the window ledge, but I couldn't make things right. I wanted to go back to that last day sitting across from each other. I'd spill the truth about everything and she'd tell me how to handle it, without seeming to. And then I'd play something she loved, something elegant and difficult, like her. And she'd see how I hadn't let my chops get ruined by that crass casino of mine.

I had agreed to fill in at the Crescendo that night — a half-assed attempt to get my mind off things. They called the condo about 11 in the evening and Honey drove out to the casino to break the news to me.

I had about twenty minutes left and I saw her come in, sit down, order a drink. I tried a Billie Holiday number that night, "You Go to My Head," but just the piano arrangement. I didn't have the balls to sing it. Someone had requested "You Send Me" so I made my way through that, preoccupied, and then joined her at the bar.

She handed me a double shot of scotch. I think I'd known my mother was dead all through my last number. Honey never came to see me work, and if she did, she never would have worn an old windbreaker thrown over a T-shirt and pair of washed-out jeans. Ryan, the bartender, poured the drink into a paper cup, and we drove to the care facility, rode the elevator up to room 416, and said goodbye even though she was already gone, because that's what you do.

You might have thought that I'd be incapable of feeling anything but despair that night, that I would yearn for nothing more than the merciful oblivion of sleep. I think Honey thought so too, because she did everything but brew up some hot chocolate and read me a bedtime recipe.

But that's not what I wanted. I wanted her, exactly as she'd shown me how to want her every night since that first time, except that now despair blended with desire and I ached to be driven, forcibly if necessary, out of my mind. She understood and took me there.

10.

THE LAST THURSDAY IN NOVEMBER I played a double set at the Crescendo, 6 p.m. to 12 a.m. — a list of holiday favorites and pop along with a bit of smooth jazz. I was distracted all evening because Honey had been campaigning for the two of us to get away, fly off on some kind of holiday. Or as she put it, "It's been a fucking horrible run of bad luck. Let's go see if we can shake things up in Vegas." When I asked if she thought all those glittering streets and gambling halls could be an antidote to a fucking horrible run of bad luck she said she didn't see how it could hurt and went ahead and booked a flight for early December. "Seven long days at a garish, overpriced hotel in the heart of fantasy-land," she said, and reminded me that we never had to leave the hotel, if that's what I wanted. Our room had an expansive view of the endless desert — like a big blank screen. We could switch Vegas on or leave it off.

At intermission that night I noticed that she had called my cell around 8, so I dialed her back. It rang four times and then went to voicemail. I tried her again later during a break, no answer; I figured she'd gone to bed and didn't want to wake her.

All the way back to the condo that night I thought about Vegas. I decided she was right. How could it hurt to visit an adult playground for a week? It might be a treat to walk around a casino, the real thing, without working. I started to get into the idea, rather than just go along.

Havenhurst was the usual black column against the night sky. I didn't expect any lights because of the late hour, so I was surprised to see an amber square floating on the fifth floor. I pictured her wrapped in the comforter, watching a movie and waiting for me — one of my own all-time favorite "studies" of her, matted and framed and forever hung up in my mind.

The comforter was the first thing I saw when I came through the door. But Honey wasn't in it. It lay on the floor in a heap next to the kitchen. She sat a few feet away, on the sofa, dressed as she had been when I left that evening. She stared at the mound with an expectant look and didn't break her gaze until I sat down, touched her shoulder, and asked what was going on.

Her eyes went over my face, her mouth struggling to shape a response. I started to get up, thinking to throw the blanket back and reassure her that whatever was under the comforter, whatever she'd broken, could easily be replaced, but she grabbed my arm and pulled me down next to her.

"Don't," she said. She tried to say something more, gave up, then took my arm and we walked over together. I reached toward the blanket as if to pull it back but she stopped me. "I'll do it," she said. "It should be me."

A man lay underneath with what appeared to be — what's the word for a wound like that? Or was it two wounds? Or three? I couldn't tell. Blood spread over the parquet floor and pooled along the length his body. He wore a pair of khakis and a brown suede jacket and looked to be about forty or so, heavy-set, shaved head and a close-clipped goatee.

"He's dead, isn't he?" Honey said, a fact so obvious you could only miss it if you were in a different house on another street in a distant town. I pressed my fingers to his neck. His shocked eyes no longer registered any of the agony he must have felt at the height of . . . whatever happened.

I covered the body and led her back to the sofa. Blood soaked the left leg of her jeans. She had a stain on her neck as well. And welts above her collarbones. I licked my sleeve and dabbed away at the blood on her neck and then gave up and ran some water through a tea towel in the kitchen and brought it back to her. When I asked her what happened, who this man was, she looked at me, at him, and away.

She touched her ear. "Gold stud," she said. "He came by just after you left for work. I thought it was you at the door, you'd for-gotten something, so I opened up and in he came." She stood up, seemed to forget why — and sat back down again.

"He said he wanted me back and wouldn't take no. I reminded him of our deal, all the money paid back. He said that was bull-shit. He'd only agreed so that he could see me again. The $20,000 couldn't have hurt either, I reminded him. He ignored that and went on about how much he loved me. He said that if I came back I could have anything I wanted, whatever the terms — as if I was some kind of bank transaction, which, let's face it, I was." She pressed her hands to her face. "Jesus, Nic. He must have had someone checking up on me because it was obvious he knew about you. He started right in talking shit. 'When's lover-girl expected home? How about we party a little, the three of us — like the old days.'" She looked at me, pained, and apologized, as if her racy past was the worst thing of all. "When I told him to go fuck himself he cornered me in the kitchen and put his hands around my throat. Like this." The sight of her hands covering the welts on her own neck was too much. I pulled them away.

"I felt the throb in my temples," she said, "and heard myself choking. I thought, *This is how I'm going to die: at the hands of this mean bastard.* And I just couldn't allow it. I tried to grab a knife out of the block but knocked it over and they all clattered into the sink. So I let him have it with the block and he let go."

That's when she remembered the gun in the back of the junk drawer, crammed in behind the lightbulbs and screwdrivers. I couldn't recall seeing it there myself. I wondered if I'd ever seen that gun at all. It was almost like a pistol from a movie, and yes, I'd seen the movie but not all the props. I wished she'd gotten rid of it after her mother's death, but then I thought about what might have happened if she had.

"He stood there raving about how if I didn't pack my bags, he'd wait for you to get home, kill the two of us, and then himself. Ordinarily I would have made some smart-ass comment — you know, would you consider reversing the order? But he was high and drunk. And he started on about how he knew someone was following him, the cops, or somebody with fucked-up intentions, or both. He said he'd bought plane tickets. And then he had a closer look at the gun and started laughing. 'Not that old piece of shit again,' he said. Then he opened a few buttons on his shirt and invited me to go ahead and shoot him because if I thought that piece of crap could blow a hole bigger than a BB gun I was crazy. He said I was beginning to remind him of my lunatic mother."

She got up and began pacing between Aurbuck's body and the kitchen, then sat down carefully, as if she wasn't sure the couch would really be there.

"And Nic? He looked me straight in the eye, the cold bastard, all the while laughing that stupid jerk laugh of his. And he said, 'That deranged cunt of a mother of yours must have had to squeeze off three shots just to get the job done.'"

She stared at the comforter. I stared at her. I'm not sure how much time went by. I could feel her grow calm, or something resembling that, as I got more anxious waiting for her to fill in the blank, which she did in the most quiet, steady way imaginable — almost as if the whole terrible event grew ever-smaller in her mind, a tainted kind of blessing, and it was all she could do to call it up for review.

"And I *told* him. I said, 'Call me anything you want, because god knows I deserve it. But leave my mother out of it.'"

Four, six, ten seconds passed as I waited for her to state the obvious, as if none of it had really happened unless she said it; as if there was still some chance the guy had suddenly realized what an asshole he was and shot himself — three times.

"And that's when I shot him."

I dug my cell phone out of my jacket, my hands shaking. She asked what I was doing. "I'm calling the police."

She took the phone from my hand and placed it on the coffee table. "We can't call the police, Nic," she whispered.

"But this was self-defense. Or the thing might have gone off on its own. That gun was an accident waiting to happen. And now it's happened!"

It was as if she didn't hear me. She said the cops would find out about their relationship and assume she killed him to ensure that he didn't drag her into his testimony during whatever investigation he'd been going on about.

"The kind of stuff I was involved in? I'll be in jail by Thursday. All the old shit was coming home to roost. He wanted me to run away with him. I told you: I was just as fucking horrible as he was." She said she knew a thing or two about short-term incarceration and wasn't going back for the long version.

"But you didn't *murder* him," I said.

"It doesn't matter! I was all heated up, and the gun didn't just go off. I knew what I was doing. Let's at least not bullshit ourselves."

"He attacked you. It's self-defense, or manslaughter maybe, that's all there is to it!"

"I slaughtered a so-called man, alright. I pulled the trigger three times! Look at him. He's a fucking mess." I couldn't argue there. "And if you help me stand him up," she added, "I'll do it again."

A comment like that? You'd have to be dead not to feel the horrifying chill. But then I looked again at the way he defiled her neck. I remembered the pearl at her throat that first night we made love, my fingers on the chain's clasp, her lips against my ear whispering, No, leave it on . . . and how she kissed me with the pearl on her tongue.

"Here's what I want you to do," she said and began moving about the kitchen searching through drawers. "I want you to pack your stuff — as much as you can. Throw everything in your dad's Chevy and go straight back to Montague Street. Don't call. Don't email. Don't contact me at all, for a long time. I'll get in touch with you when the time is right. I promise."

"What the hell are you talking about?"

"I appreciate your loyalty, Nic. But you didn't sign up for this."

"And you did?"

She grabbed the front of my parka. "I'm telling you to get the hell out."

"I'm telling you I'm not going anywhere," I said and kissed her hard, if only to stop her talking.

We both sat back down on the couch and stared at the heap. I know this is going to sound crazy but I couldn't help thinking of Honey and me at the Saturday matinee back in the day; the two of us front row center, our chins tipped up, the light and shadows from the big screen rippling over our big eyes. The only thing missing was the popcorn and the music rising up to the climax and then eventually (and most important) that towering *THE END*. There had to be an end at some point, didn't there? A moment when we would stagger out into the afternoon sunlight?

We sat there in silence for maybe ten minutes. Then we both got up and started collecting the articles required to get rid of a body. And it all seemed so natural in an eerie, dazed and awful way. We might have been setting the table for lunch.

We rolled him into the comforter and wrapped him round and round with packing tape before Honey realized we'd forgotten to fish the car keys out of his jacket. So we untaped him, rolled him all the way back the other way and started over.

"Now what?" I asked after we finished, not really wanting to know, just trying to catch my breath. And who knows, maybe she'd changed her mind about calling the police.

"Now?" she said, tossing the tape and scissors back in the junk drawer. "Now we take a long, blissfully quiet cruise to the lake with my man."

There were only three cars out in the lot — mine, the Eldorado, and Aurbuck's — but we loaded him down the stairway rather than risk meeting some guy in the elevator returning home from a late shift out on the highway. I waited by the delivery door while Honey brought his car around, a sports car with a trunk so small we couldn't get it closed with him in it, so we laid him out on his back seat instead, squeezed the door closed, and then Honey started driving.

I followed her in the Chevy to a secluded inlet at Fortune Bay, far enough north that a sheet of ice had already formed. Honey drove the car right up to the edge — so close that she couldn't have backed out if she tried. The two of us slipped around in the snow and mud, heaving from behind while the tiny car clung to shore as if it knew what lay ahead. When it finally let go and rolled onto the lake, the ice fractured into thick puzzle pieces all around its body. The water, a murky slush, lapped its windows — the sound of a good-sized bottle submerged in a massive sink. It floated for a minute or so and disappeared. Silence under the stars.

I don't think I realized how much she hated him until she whispered, "Fucking waste of an MG," and threw the car keys after him.

They skidded across the ice and stopped about four yards out. We stood there looking at them for a few seconds as the snow filtered down through the pines, not sure what to do, or if we ought to do anything. Honey threw a few rocks after the keys, which either missed or broke through the ice and disappeared. She'd forgotten her gloves, so took off her toque and wrapped it around her hands to keep them warm. I asked her if she thought the freeze would come before anyone found the body, which I had to think was the strangest question I'd ever ask in my life.

"Maybe if we found a long enough branch we could sweep the keys back," I suggested. Because the look of them lying there . . .

"Fortune Bay's a hideous backwater that no one in their right mind would bother visiting in a million years," she said. "And this is the snow belt. There'll be ten inches on top of those keys, his car, and that asshole by the end of the month." She yanked her toque back on. "Well, at least now he really *is* an ex," she said, and we drove home to Buckthorn in my father's Chevy.

Back at the condo we cleaned up the mess in the kitchen, the blood on the floor, and undressed, not a word between us, and got in the shower. I stood with my arms wrapped around myself watching traces of what I imagined was Aurbuck's blood, along with muck from the bay, slip down her body. And then I closed my eyes and blocked it out. I saw her in the showers at school instead, back in the days when she smelled like cinnamon toast and apples, and the only stain on our hands was grease from a broken bike chain. She reached out, guided me to her, passed the soap over my body. I washed her hair.

For days afterwards, unless I'd had a drink, I couldn't stop picturing my fingers on Aurbuck's neck, no pulse beneath them. I would have sworn I still smelled his awful cologne on my hands.

Yes, I thought, *I've got some dirt on me now.*

II.

I THOUGHT THE VEGAS TRIP was off because — to summarize a long, agonizing, half-inebriated debate — who pushes a car with a body into a lake and goes on holiday?

"You might be surprised," Honey said.

Her lack of remorse shocked me. I didn't like to imagine what else might have passed between her and Aurbuck, all the things she may be refusing to tell me. On the other hand, she suggested, maybe we should think of it as a well-placed period of time away from the neighborhood, rather than a vacation. "A dish of lurid sherbet before the return to overcooked meat and potatoes," was how she put it.

So, the following Thursday, first week of December, we packed, got dressed, and splurged on an airport limo to Torrent to catch the flight to Vegas. The two of us were wrecks, in our own way, but we didn't talk about it, just focused on getting somewhere else. About thirty miles from the city it started to snow those wet, ragged flakes that join together and slide off the windshield in a mass.

She sipped from her flask and checked her phone a lot, concerned, she said, that the flight might be canceled. I didn't worry at all. It was as if there were so many concerns whirling around in my head that I couldn't pick a favorite. The overload, and a couple of sips from her flask, made me numb. Her cell rang once or twice, but she said she didn't recognize the number so let it alone. "Now's hardly the time to chat with strangers," she said.

Time seemed to slow down as the 727 lifted up and away. I turned in my seat to watch the city lights and traffic on the highway heading north and south — a stream of red one way, a chain of white glitter the other. And then the squares of dark earth; the wild, uncultivated fields to the west; the forests filling up with snow; the cold, deep, lonely lakes up around Buckthorn County and farther north. I squinted through the window as if I might see Fortune Bay slide past, the MG bobbing in the dark, icy depths with you know who inside. I turned away.

After we leveled off the flight attendant came down the aisle with the drinks cart and Honey relaxed. She ordered a shot of bourbon on the rocks. I'd had more sips from her flask than I'd planned and declined. Three thousand feet began to feel transcendent in a way it never had before, not that I'd flown often, just a couple of trips east as a teen to compete in piano recitals or provide accompaniment. We were above it all, if only for a few hours.

Honey seemed her old self, her eyes soft and warm as the whiskey in her glass. She pressed her knee against mine and asked if I remembered the part in *Gilda* where she goes off partying with some guy she just met and tortures her old lover by saying, "If I were a ranch they would have named me the Bar None." We shared a boisterous laugh about that one, and then low-keyed it, not wishing to draw attention. "Kiss me," she whispered and pointed to that tender spot just below her ear.

She took off her coat, a dark pea jacket she bought at the Sears close-out sale, something versatile, she said, to keep her toasty through the hellish winter. Underneath she wore a silk top and a light sweater to fend off the airplane chill. A guy across the aisle watched her fingers slip the first three buttons of the sweater free and then stared at her legs. When he looked at me I winked — I don't have a clue what came over me — and he blushed and looked away.

I imagined him after disembarking the plane, his route through the city in a cab, business meetings by day, gambling and drinking along the Strip at night. Two or three months later, settled into real life again, the woman on the plane would come back to him, just as she had come back to me: her low whisper, her beautiful fingers on the buttons of her sweater — that laugh.

The chauffeur lifted our suitcases from the trunk and led us through the bright, blinding entranceway of the Grand Hotel into a foyer the size of a tennis court smothered in scarlet broadloom. As Honey signed in, I squinted into the shadowy interior of the place: the sounds of roulette wheels and slot machines and dice scrambling across reaches of hushed grass-green, all laced with the tinkling of glasses and murmured conversation, now and then the sound of a distant piano.

Up we went in the elevator, the two of us staring at the vague outlines of ourselves in its black marble walls shot through with gold and polished to a sheen. When we let ourselves into the room I felt as though I'd stepped off a platform and into the sky. I even latched onto Honey for a moment, who kept her legs.

We were up high — thirty floors — and the suite was all tall windows and glass and shiny floors. The furniture seemed shifting, hard to pinpoint, and I realized this was because most of it was made of acrylic, even the dining table and chairs, right down to the placemats, which could have been cut from a bolt of mirage. The only color was violent splashes of scarlet poppies in white vases, a sofa with chrome legs and red leather cushions. There was a dizzying outdoor terrace accessed through a set of sliding glass doors, and an adjoining sun room with rattan lounges and overstuffed cushions and two or three planters with miniature palms plus a few other exotic plants I didn't know — none of them would have survived Buckthorn. I hadn't wondered until then (after all, we'd been so busy) how the heck she was paying for all that opulence. She hadn't asked me to chip in. When I told her I had every intention of doing so she laughed and explained how she'd won the Vegas holiday draw at the bank.

"I thought I told you! It's practically a freebie, I just called ahead and changed the bank's lame booking for a decent room."

"Decent?"

"You just have to ask the right questions in the right manner. It's not even the very best suite. That one was occupied. Look, don't worry about anything. It's all squared away. We'll just relax and have a fine old time at the bank's expense."

I followed her into the bedroom and we threw the suitcases on the floor because the fancy bed seemed to whisper *don't you dare.* The thing was massive and round with a pink silk comforter, black satin sheets, and two white end tables on either side. We exchanged a smirk regarding the boudoir's hackneyed but expensive décor, unpacked a few things, and Honey "reconnoitered" while I undressed to take a shower. The bathroom was also huge, and the one truly separate room in the place. The overall sheen and polish continued: the marble floor, the tiled walls with a variety of brass faucets and nozzles fixed to them.

I twisted a few of the spigots, got in, and had a good long cry about my mother, my father, Inez, what Honey and I had probably gotten ourselves into with Aurbuck — everything. It was satisfying and violent, what with the force of all that water coming at me: a real hurricane of grief.

In the days to come Honey would decide she didn't fancy the shower and opt instead for bathing. "Are you kidding me? All that hardware? I'll bet it's like being blown off a cruise ship crossing the North Sea and living to tell the tale."

"Please don't tell the tale," I said.

I wrapped a towel around me and took my time as I regained my composure, examined the bathroom amenities, as they called them: creams and lotions in a variety of fruit flavors, a body wash and repair kit, loofahs and four rolls of thick white face cloths to match the bath and hand towels. Then I pulled on one of the hotel robes (white, with fancy gold lettering over the pocket) and wandered back out to our platform in the sky.

Honey stood on the terrace with her back to me, her phone pressed to her ear, the city spread out beyond. It seemed an endless shimmering sea of candy-colored lights. Except that it did eventually end — and suddenly, as I had seen very well when we had dropped through the clouds that night and circled the airport a few times before cleared to land: the lights of the strip, the hotels, towers, fountains, all kinds of amusements and distractions I'd never get to the bottom of — and then the desert darkness (the true endless part) spread out beyond. I felt as though we were in the center of a sort of sargasso sea of lights floating uneasily in the night, or lost in the innards of an immense computer board.

She turned, smiled, and walked back into the suite, sliding the glass door closed behind her. "Checking tomorrow's weather," she said and dropped her phone onto the dining table, that phantom-type thing you might have thought would support nothing but air. When I asked what was in the forecast she pulled me close, kissed my neck, and dried the tips of my hair with the robe's collar.

"Look how your hair curls against your neck right there," she said. "All these years I've known you and I never saw that."

She'd taken to pointing out things about me that she found charming or sexy, which embarrassed and thrilled me at the same time. I had certain assets it seemed, things I never thought about myself. She made me feel confident, somehow, as though I could slip into a different version of myself (or a different life) like one of those luxurious hotel robes.

When she untied my robe a warm breeze seemed to pass through me. Every inch of my body opened to her, all on its own, without any help at all from my mind, which couldn't have done anything about it anyway.

"I know this is going to be impossible," she whispered. "But let's do everything we can to forget all about time for the next seven days."

When she let me go I felt my knees go too, and I had to sink down on one of those tricky ghost chairs. But then she came back with that tiny brass ashtray with the mother-of-pearl lid. She said she had a fabulous idea.

"Let's draw the drapes, get high, and wreck the bed," she said. When I laughed and insisted that I already *was* high and wrecked, she kneeled in front of me and took the collar of my robe in her hands. "You know, Nic, sometimes I think you believe we're all born with some kind of impenetrable pleasure ceiling and you've already reached yours. Let's see about that, okay?"

She said my hair smelled like a summer storm, like it had in the old days when we rode home on our bikes with the rain in our eyes.

12.

WE TOOK CARE of the first three days by never leaving the suite. Or rather, Honey left once to buy a pair of sunglasses in the boutique on the ground floor: cat-eyes with rhinestones — what else? When I asked her to model them for me she said, "Oh I plan to, I assure you." But then she couldn't find them in that minuscule purse of hers. "Only you could lose a pair of glasses in an elevator," I told her. We ordered room service, watched movies on the big screen, lolled around in our bathrobes, picking away at gourmet pizza and sushi. Often we read aloud to each other from an assortment of complimentary magazines and brochures while we drank Chardonnay all afternoon. (Red we saved for evening, whenever that might occur. The borders in Vegas seemed . . . tenuous.)

Listen to this, I said, as we lay sunning ourselves on the terrace: *Bodies: The Exhibition: Over 200 preserved human body specimens in dramatic action poses. The MGM Grand Lion Habitat: Watch lions play right in the heart of Vegas; Indoor Skydiving, complete with 120 mph wind; Tour the Grand Canyon by helicopter; The Mandalay Shark Reef; Big Elvis, a 700-lb impersonator who could be found at Bill's Gamblin' Hall and Saloon.*

She lay on her back wearing one of the hotel's eye masks to blot out the light — black satin, which made her look like Zorro relaxing on her day off. A dismantled newspaper lay under her lounge along with the scattered peel from that morning's orange. As usual, she came out with several comments and wisecracks: "Skydiving in a 120 mile per hour wind? Ouch! I guess it's not the naked kind." Or: "A 700-pound Elvis *might* be found? How the fuck could you possibly miss the guy?"

"And here's a good one," I said. "*Mandalay Shark Reef,* 1,300,000 gallons of water swarming with predators. Should we go?"

"No."

"Why not?"

Even the eye mask couldn't hide the droll look that came over her face whenever she hit on another old movie favorite. "Because we can *never* go back to Manderley again, Rebecca. You know that."

As for Honey's reading material, she enjoyed quoting from articles about different spirits, especially wine appreciation. *Most rosé wines are ephemeral and should be consumed young. But this is not always true.* "Ah, ha," she said, winked at me and continued. *A small number of serious rosés age and evolve beautifully, like some of the great Provençal rosés of Bandol, the idiosyncratic rosé of Château Simone from the appellation of Palette, also in Provence, and the equally distinctive rosé of Valentini from Abruzzo, Italy.*

"How freaking luscious is that?" she said. I didn't know whether she was referring to the content of the article or the texture of the words on her tongue. Her pronunciation was excellent, as far as I could tell, and the way she read I couldn't help longing to savor every letter myself, never mind the wine.

"I think we should go live somewhere really old while we're still young," she said. "Some fascinating, remarkable place. Let's rent a villa with a strange phrase of some kind engraved over its door — something worth saying, an ancient vow or warning of some kind — and who cares if neither of us knows what the hell it means. And we'll have a courtyard with olive trees and marble statues of beautiful, broken women, and goddamn weeds poking through the cracks everywhere, splitting everything apart in the most violent and fantastic way. Let's care about things like seasoning the earthenware pot and using the right chef knife. We'll grow piles of herbs and spend hours stirring the sauce pot and linger a long time over every fucking thing."

"Of course, yes. Let's do it." I agreed because how could I do anything else, once she got going, once she grabbed my hand and dragged me away from myself? And I meant it. I would have thrown the old life away and vanished with her that night, or day, even if I wasn't drunk on wine, on her, on everything. After all, I'd stuffed a guy into an MG and pushed him into a lake with her. I assumed she was speaking of that island dreamland of hers, and if so, then I was ready to become enamored of Elba too. What the hell? Maybe we'd *both* been born there in the life that counts.

"And there has to be a hand-pump in the courtyard, so we can splash our feet with cold water all through summer," I offered. "And I'll wash the salt out of your hair when we get back from the beach."

"Here's to lemons, almonds, ripe pears —"

"And sea breezes. And tangled sheets every morning."

"Oh god, yes," she said. "To our ruined bed." She was sitting up by then, the mask pushed back into her hair.

And then I made her promise that even if things didn't happen exactly the way we described she would never forget us. I wasn't yet aware of how necessary the human capacity to forget really is, and how merciful. She patted the lounge beside her and when I got there (three seconds) folded me into the thick warmth of her bathrobe. Her body's scent, that top-notch cologne owned by no one but her, mingled with the perfume of that morning's vanished orange. A bit of newspaper ink stained her knuckles.

"Hell no, Nic. I won't forget. I haven't found one thing in this godawful fucked-up world that compares to you."

Every time I turned around it was cocktail hour. I began to feel that our getaway was in Vegas, sure, but also some kind of boozing bootcamp, which probably really existed somewhere among all the Sin City craziness. I pictured the two of us wading through white water with two bourbons and a party tray held high above our heads, our khaki rucksacks packed with all the paraphernalia required for wilderness survival: corkscrew, shaker, strainer, ice bucket, shot glass — not that Honey ever measured out the booze.

Three days of cocktails, hangovers, room service, an endless loop of oldies at what Honey called the indoor drive-in, and on top of that long nights, and days, of sex that made me feel as if I'd slipped some kind of tether and floated free of myself. I had no words for what amounted to a series of sexual hangovers which were, in their own way, as unsettling as those induced by too much alcohol. Some nights, after what seemed like hours of lovemaking, I would wake in the night, or day, and for a few awful seconds forget that Honey had come back into my life, or ever kissed me. And then my head would get going on my mother, my father, Inez — and the snow falling on the MG in Fortune Bay.

But then she'd wake up too and pull me against her. And all those crazy fantasies she shared with me — the azure seas, the sailboats, the marble ruins and those questions that lost themselves in the asking — flooded into me and stained my head back into a deep, blue calm.

By the time day four rolled around, we agreed it was time to get out of there — get dressed, walk around, eat a proper meal. We had gorged ourselves on each other while merely snacking on actual food and were thin and famished, wrung out like greedy lovers who, try as they may, can't get to the bottom of their hunger for each other. And I guess the story goes that such lovers are doomed to flame out, go down in disappointment and ashes, but I knew that would never be our story. Because to sit next to her in a packed café, or feel her knee pressed against mine in the back of a cab, or listen to her laugh as a fake gondolier drifted down Las Vegas Boulevard — that was all I needed. And why, if achieving this kind of heaven was so easy, should our feelings ever be revoked, or ruined? Because who needed the pearly gates, and angels with trumpets, and everlasting life? All those divine promises down the road? These, if they existed, had to be out of reach to us now, and I'd die before I repented anything about her. So I'd settle for simply hanging around her for the rest of this life, while she moved about performing small adjustments to the everyday — the way she lined herself up while seated in a chair, chin in hand, the grace of her crossed legs, a few strands of hair eluding the ever-present elastic she had somehow transformed into something that, it seemed to me, would endure forever, like one of those objects of personal adornment you see under glass at a museum and stand there stricken, somehow, and never more alive.

We sorted through our suitcases, still half-packed, looking for the nicest stuff from our wardrobe, a few combinations that worked for the jobs back in Buckthorn and might serve in Vegas too. Honey had the edge in the fashion department, but she was always willing to share.

Have I conveyed her elegance — she would have scoffed at the term — when she gathered up her hair and slipped a plastic chopstick from the debris of yesterday's takeout into it, the fine hairs under her raised arms, her beautiful hands as she slipped her sandals on — the same hands that could, among other things, push a man's car into the lake (with him in it), toss away his keys, and remain incapable of a false move, a clumsy gesture.

After we were all set to go she pulled me close, drawing me into one of those notorious movie lines that I thought I'd tire of someday but never did.

"Maybe you shouldn't dress like that," she said. I picked up on it easily: a Ned Racine line to Matty Walker, the seductive, conniving femme fatale in *Body Heat*. I could hardly pass up such a meaty part, under the circumstances.

"It's just a blouse and skirt. I don't know what you're talking about."

"Then you shouldn't wear that body," she whispered next to my ear. And then the usual, yet so unusual, happened and we had to get dressed all over again.

140

Two hours later off we went, blinking and shading our eyes in the harsh desert light. We had thought it was dusk and were going for dinner, but in fact the sun was rising, not setting. We laughed and altered course.

We took a cab to The Egg & I on West Sahara Avenue, a diner I'd read about in the brochures, and there we devoured man-sized servings of eggs benny, French toast, extra sides of fries. Honey said we probably looked like our car had broken down a month ago and we'd just staggered in, starving from the desert. "That's how I feel," I said.

We sat at a table next to a giant mural that I thought looked like something straight out of Buckthorn County before everything went downhill; imagine that, coming all this way: big sky with puffy white clouds and a farm pasture, red brick house, truck rumbling by in the foreground, a lake minus an MG with a dead body inside tucked into the forest behind.

Afterwards we caught another cab back to our neck of the woods and strolled down to the Bellagio fountains, then browsed the 40,000-foot Bonanza gift shop on Las Vegas Boulevard.

"What fantastic, tacky shit," Honey said, delighted. "Can you imagine my mother here?"

"Can you imagine mine?" We drew a bit of attention to ourselves yukking it up over that one, and then, you know, wanting to cry.

She was wearing a pair of Elvis mirror sunglasses with slick dark sideburns attached to them when her phone rang. She swore and said she meant to leave the damn phone back at the suite.

"Fucking telemarketers have followed me all the way to Vegas. *I saw what you did, and I know who you are*," she whispered into the phone, another classic midnight movie line from our youth, and hung up. She asked what I thought of her new look and I admitted that sideburns looked just as alluring on her as they did on the King.

The following day we rose late, had breakfast in our suite, watched a movie, and then about 5 o'clock Honey said she might go down to the hotel casino and gawk at the high rollers. She didn't say *we* should go down, but that's because I needed a nap. I hadn't slept well the previous evening; up half the night worrying and wandering around the absentees — my name for all that acrylic furniture, which was even harder to see in the dark.

When I woke later and swept the bedroom drapes aside, that glittering Vegas nighttime panorama lay stretched out on the horizon once again, and then fell off into darkness. My phone said 8 p.m. — three hours since Honey had left, so I called her. No answer. Maybe she'd decided to lay some bets and turned it off so she could concentrate or couldn't hear over the racket and commotion of all that cash being gambled away.

I dressed and went looking for her.

Thirty minutes of aimless wandering left me stymied. I called her again. Nothing. So I continued revolving under the faux-starry sky, the playing cards fanning and folding, the neon hubbub broken by pockets of cool, silent shade.

Apart from the high-roller rooms and the poor folk gambling areas, the casino had a bunch of restaurants and compact eateries, as well as two party-clubs, one at ground level and the other on the twenty-first floor. I toured all of them, with an odd, dreamy sense that everything — the eating, gambling, and losing — took place not in a casino but in a wreck at the bottom of the sea, and any minute the windows would implode and the ocean would leave us drifting through the rooms, all splayed out in our fancy clothes, the stars twinkling merrily overhead.

I called her again, got peeved, and then thought to hell with it, I'd have a drink in the Amber Room, the ground floor club. I vowed to let the phone ring if she called me, and she could stew and fret for a change, but I knew I wouldn't, that I'd pick up right away.

Concave mirrors lined the curved walls of the circular bar all the way round the perimeter of the dance floor from entrance to exit, though both were a challenge to find again once you were stuck in the deep, thumping heart of the place. Ten or so "mixologists" in gleaming white shirts and caramel colored bowties kept busy over their beakers, blending an array of fantastical cocktails, the racks above their heads lined with oddly shaped glasses, like the interior of a fractured geode.

I stood at the bar, midway into the curve, watching the dancers move to the rhythm of a Latin beat as splinters of miniature rainbows spangled the darkness. Then the tune dropped and segued into one of those lush disco numbers Inez loved, the backbeat first, a little guitar, and then a whole brass section coming up behind, and whatever else Donna Summer needed to get things going first thing in the morning over at the Ramones'.

I didn't recognize her at first. I don't know why, because it goes without saying I would have known her anywhere. The same blue shift. That little purse with the narrow strap across her body. She was dancing. My mind went back to her and me dancing to the old records we played on my grandmother's old turntable. I was just about to join her when the music transitioned to something slower and I realized what had thrown me: she had a dance partner.

She seemed self-conscious with the guy at first, and that was unlike her; so confident in her body, so fluid in every movement, but now hesitant, though never awkward, in this man's arms — until she slipped out of them again, the song changing to a slow jive. Several shadowy figures revolved around them, like cold, dark planets in comparison to her lightness, her casual beauty. Even her tentative movements, the way her hand eluded his as she moved away, her little mistakes, only emphasized her physical grace. She knew her instrument, and — how should I put it — how to improvise error into a kind of magic that was so much better than perfection. She always had.

I ordered a scotch and drank it down quick, and then stood gazing at my face in the mirror behind the bar, now blue, then violet, then streaked with tainted gold. I felt as though a hundred hours had passed before she joined me, breathless.

She called me several times, she said, and then assumed I'd turned the phone off, or couldn't hear it over the noise. "It's lousy reception in here anyway."

"I've been looking for you everywhere," I said. "And then I came down here and had a couple of drinks because, frankly, I was pissed with you."

"Come on," she said and took my arm. "Let's get the hell out of here before twinkletoes comes back for another spin around the dance floor."

In the elevator we didn't speak all the way up. But no sooner had the door closed behind us than she pulled me close and kissed me — my mouth, my neck, and back again — her hands in my hair.

I thought she had made me feel everything by then, or at least more than I ever dreamed, and now we'd just start over again and travel down familiar terrain into a kind of expected bliss, the assumed euphoric refrain. But that night I realized there might be no end to where she could take me.

The day before our departure, we packed, ate a quick bite in the Paradise Grill on the ground floor and were back in the room by late afternoon. Honey poured us a brandy and we sat on the terrace and watched the sun begin to set. She said it looked like a ripe peach rolling off a cracked blue plate. Why cracked, I don't know, but she was right. A few stars appeared, bright pin pricks along the desert horizon.

As far as I knew we'd both avoided news updates from home and stayed true, at least on the surface, to leaving that whole surreal situation behind for the week. Both of us seemed hesitant to acknowledge that in a few hours we would touch down in the too real world once again, from lurid sherbet to overcooked meat and potatoes — and then some.

We sat in silence, and then she surprised me by asking if I thought I'd ever get married. I didn't even think to answer her seriously, just laughed, because I'd never thought of myself as much of a catch and told her so.

"Oh, but that's not true," she said. Silence again, while I thought things over and realized that because of my parents' deaths I owned a house — ramshackle, but still — and an insurance policy payout. I'd never thought about it beyond helping Honey with the $20,000, which as far as I was concerned she could keep. In my heart I hoped she'd agree to move in with me someday. So what if Montague Street wasn't as sexy as Elba? We could still have all the things we talked about. But in our good old horrible hometown? Who was I kidding?

"You're sweet, honest, attractive as hell — and loyal," she said. "Well, we know all about that, don't we?" She squeezed my hand and took a sip of brandy. "I'm the one who's not much of a catch, if you want to get right down to it."

I pointed out that all the assets she'd named of mine were really hers.

"Why, thank you, darling," she said and took an extravagant draw on the ghost of a cigarette. "But no. I'm a liability. Case in point." She raised her glass and finished the brandy.

"What are you saying?"

"Come on, Nic. Haven't you noticed? I'm practically an alcoholic."

"You like to drink, so what? It's Vegas. Isn't that why people come here?"

"To drink, gamble, and get fucked. You're right. But that doesn't change the fact that I was a boozer in training at eight or nine, and a raging success by eighteen. A real whiskey virtuoso."

"It seems to me you can stop drinking whenever you want. Most of the time you're sober, after all. You're not reeling around drunk at the bank and knocking down the interest rates in your biscotti dress shirt."

"Oh, Nic, I adore you but you're so goddamn naive. I think you'd have to see me in a straightjacket before you believed I was a lush; me having visions of little roosters with straw hats coming through the keyholes, like that guy in *The Lost Weekend*. Of course I'm not plastered all the time. It's all about capacity and timing and being a top-notch liar. Stick around though. You never know, there might be a few barnyard birds on the horizon."

"I don't find that funny," I said.

She apologized and looked away. I got up, walked to the railing, and leaned there for a couple minutes, before turning back to her.

"Do you know what it would do to me if . . . ?" I started over. Because I didn't want her to think of me as weak and soppy, on top of being so-called naive. "Remember when you taught me how to jive in my bedroom?"

"'A Lover's Concerto,'" she said.

"That's right. You slowed it right down for me. We were eleven, twelve. I was stiff and self-conscious, not graceful and easy like you. I still play that song now and then at my rotten job, when I can stand to hear myself sing it. Mostly I stick to the classical version. It's not that I've come to hate it. How could I? It's just that I'd been waiting too long for a specific vignette to unfold, a certain moment I see in my mind. I look up from the keyboard one night, as the casino door opens — cue the slow ceiling fan, the bluesy sax riff, pull in close on the piano player's hands — and the girl who waltzed out of my life at eighteen waltzes back in . . ."

I sat back down next to her, certain I'd blown it with that horrible sentimental side of myself I'd inherited from the old man. But why stop now? I took her hand and pressed a kiss into her palm.

"I've been in love with you . . . all my life," I said. "Marry me."

We tied the knot at the Love Me Tender wedding chapel on Las Vegas Boulevard that very night (open twenty-four hours, like everything else in Vegas.)

I wore Honey's blue shift and she my skirt with the pink blouse so that we could both feel brand new. Our rings were chosen from one of those machines with the claw you see at arcades, packed with all kinds of cheap trinkets or stuffed toys. But Love Me Tender's machine was dedicated exclusively to rings. Real knock-outs. We slid a dollar into the slot and the claw made the choice for us, "a guaranteed prize every time." Honey's was a silver bowling pin that said 2013 Ten Pin Champions and mine a gold horseshoe with white rhinestones, and inside the band read *From Hal to Tina, Luck in '92.*

A guy in a black suit and rope tie conducted the ceremony. And then Honey took me in her arms and we swayed to Elvis singing "Crying in the Chapel," which seemed to me the sultriest prayer ever set to music. I thought about trying it at the casino when I got back, and even gave it a whirl one set, but the prayer somehow failed me — I just couldn't make it through.

That night when the brides got back to their room, the first thing Honey did was throw all the booze and pot in a bag and toss it in the corner. "It's just you and me tonight, maestro," she said. "Pure as thirty acres of Buckthorn County snow." If I'd ever cared about purity and perfection, I didn't anymore. I adored her for never having bothered, even when she was riding high, to get that little chip in her front tooth fixed; the one that matched the scar on my forehead. Just a glimpse of it touched some place in me I can't explain.

The only light in the suite was the iridescent peach and blue glowing in the distance along the line of washed-out hills. We stood beside the bed and removed each other's clothes in a careful, almost hesitant way, as if we were afraid of hurting something. I felt as though I'd been high since I got to Vegas, but now I somehow felt more stoned, higher than I'd ever been. I couldn't help thinking of that day in the change room at Robinson's, and how the sight of her fingers on the buttons of her shirt undid me.

And then we fell into bed and made every kind of love — I don't mean to be crass, but if I haven't made it clear, Honey knew every composition and arrangement in the human body's song-book, from classical to jazz, to soul and gospel, to rock and Delta blues, and was a fearless improviser — until the alarm went off at daybreak.

We flew back to Torrent and had just touched down when the storm closed the airport. It took us five hours to get back to Buckthorn and I just didn't care.

If I'd thought we might never be together that way again, even stuck in a car in a snowstorm heading back to a town on the skids, even with that whole other thing waiting in the wings, I never would have gotten on that plane.

Part II

But you should know that love is also terrible.

— Carl Jung

13.

A FEW DAYS AFTER we got back to Buckthorn, Honey told me she'd be driving down to Torrent for a series of year-end bank meetings. She said she'd mentioned them on the plane. I couldn't recall, but maybe that was because I'd begun feeling anxious about our return to Buckthorn. I worried that I'd fall asleep on the flight and end up muttering, too loud, a few disjointed but incriminating phrases: *Wasted MG! Godforsaken swamp! I'll shoot him again!* So I stayed wide awake while Honey, her head on my shoulder, slept like a baby — who had knocked back three shots of whiskey.

The bank meetings would take place over three days. I wanted to drive down with her, but she convinced me to stay put. "It's a shitty business trip. I'll hardly see you. The thought of you keeping the bed warm back home is the only thing that'll keep me upright." She was adamant. "Don't worry. I'll deke out early on day three, because that's just windup bullshit anyway."

I finally gave up. It was just as well, because after she left I came down with a bug, or something, that I had probably picked up on the flight. So I bought a few groceries and settled in as the season's worst storm broke records all over the county. I ate a light dinner with a glass of wine and then went to bed early with a couple of cold tablets to help me sleep.

Maybe the combination of drugs and fever drove my dreams that night, bizarre stuff that woke me five or six times until I finally gave up, brewed myself a cup of tea, and sat down at the keyboard. I couldn't stop staring at my fingers and wondering if the same hands that pushed a guy in his sports car into a lake had the right to play something from the mind of Chopin, or anyone. I closed the piano and sat watching the wind and snow batter the windows.

That night reminded me of the winter I turned fourteen and took my first long-distance bus trip alone, up to Echo Lake for music camp: all night tucked under my jacket in that warm twilight capsule as the county's oceans of white-capped fields disappeared behind us and the pine forest rose on either side. The thought popped into my mind that Honey and I should go on a trip like that, somewhere north where the trees grow short and the landscape's strewn with those deep, tea-colored ponds you can see right to the bottom of. A person could get lost there. You might not be able to avoid it. And then I guess that thought became an idea, almost a compulsion. I blamed it on the late hour, my touch of fever, the drugs. Because for a few minutes the image of her and me on a bus traveling through the blue winter night felt so right, and every other choice so wrong, that I considered driving down to Torrent in the storm, dragging her out of that bank meeting, and insisting, "Drive with me."

I woke at 10:30 a.m. to the smell of burning coffee, the same pot I'd put on at 8 before falling back to sleep. Somebody was knocking at the door and may have been for some time.

A guy about forty-five in a dark suit and overcoat stood there. His hair, what was left of it, was auburn and his face clean-shaven and rosy from the cold. My first impulse was to decline whatever religious pamphlets he might have to offer, because it had to be way too late for redemption. But then he asked for Honey by name.

"She's not here," I said, too quickly, because I was pretty sure of what was coming. If he wasn't a neat and tidy person of faith, then he had to be the cop I'd expected to show up ever since I first laid eyes on Honey's ex tucked up under that comforter.

"I'm Detective Smith. Just up this way from the Torrent detachment." He smiled, removed his gloves, offered his hand. "And you're . . ."

"Nicole."

"Nicole . . . ?"

"Sorry, I'm Nicole Hewett." This rushed out like a sort of confession, as if I was sorry to *be* Nicole Hewett (which, at that moment . . .), so then I swung back the other way and added, "Honey's roommate?"

"Well, Nicole, I won't keep you long. Just a few moments of your time, if that's okay. I'm up this way making a few inquiries about a missing person."

"Honey's not here. And I don't think . . ." I was going to say that I doubted she'd know if a person was missing or not, and assure him that she wasn't missing herself — only at work. Or some other garbled thing. But then I rolled it back up again and added, "She'll be back."

"Okay."

"She's away on business."

"Right. Do you know when she'll return?"

"I'm not exactly sure when she'll be back. A couple of days, or three, maybe?" I hedged.

"Okay. Sure. In that case I wonder if you might let Ms. Ramone know that I'd like to talk to her. Nothing to worry about. Just a few general questions I'm asking — here and there in the neighborhood."

He handed me a card and made a few notes in one of those flip-style notebooks — god knows what notes, because how long does it take to write *Honey not home*? I stood there with the door ajar, self-conscious in the white Grand Hotel bathrobe that Honey had swiped on vacation, the little embroidered initials over the breast pocket. I got a bit giddy from nervousness then and thought about how if Honey were there she'd be laughing, even under the circumstances, about how she thought the guy was security from the Grand Hotel and had come all the way to Buckthorn to get his bathrobe back.

"I'll let you get back to your coffee," he said and pulled his gloves back on. "Have Ms. Ramone call me, will you, Nicole?" First name basis already. There was something about this guy that came across as steady and comforting, like a really good waiter but with a gun.

Yet those few seconds standing in the doorway with "the law" had to be the beginning of something bad. You know, *something bad* hot in pursuit of the *original* something bad — because it's not like I hadn't seen the movie. I had a lead role in it.

After he left I stood at the window, off to one side, and watched him walk down the sidewalk to his car and drive away. Ridiculous imaginings went through my head while I tried to double back on the obvious truth. Inquiries about a missing person? That could mean anyone at all. People had gone missing from Buckthorn for years. I should have told him there was no need to be alarmed: half of them were in Torrent and the other half were on their way to Torrent or points west, as far away from Buckthorn as they could get. I felt like throwing on my parka and chasing him down: Oh, hey! I just realized what's up. Nobody's missing! They're just en route! Then I sat down on the sofa and stared at the floor where the ghost of Aurbuck rolled up in Honey's comforter shimmered into reality once again.

I left a message on Honey's voicemail and managed to wait thirteen minutes before leaving another. By then it was 11:30, the bank meetings would be in full swing.

I threw a few things in an overnight bag and set off for Torrent.

Out on the main highway, the wind blew fierce all the way up the county line and across the acres of churned-up fields. Now and then it died away and whirling flakes hung suspended for a few seconds, and then began to fall again and merge with all the other whiteness.

Maybe it was my worried mind, my grip so hard on the wheel, that kept me on the straight and narrow rather than in the ditch like the scattering of cars I passed along the way. I stopped once for gas even though I ached to charge ahead and not let up until the Chevy's fender nudged the front desk at The Melrose on 5th, where the bank had booked rooms for its employees.

I arrived at 3:30, parked in the lot out back, and marched straight through the foyer to the front desk. They rang Honey's room but no answer. I ordered a late lunch in the hotel restaurant and pushed it around on my plate, watched the traffic go by until about 5, and then strolled around the gift shop and bought a package of Kleenex for my lousy cold. Sometime around 6 I dropped into a booth by the window in the hotel's Twilight Lounge, tossed back a couple of ibuprofen, and ordered a glass of Shiraz. At 7 I had a double scotch, and another at 8:30. I think I must have nodded off for a few minutes, long enough to wake and find my head resting against the cold window. Out on the street the holiday craziness continued — horns blared on cars whose models blurred beyond my recognition, traffic lights seemed to have taken on a sort of unique timing and pattern no longer familiar to me. Maybe it was the drinks, the medication, but I couldn't figure out how all these people made sense of the maze and got home safely. It was true that I hadn't been to the city for months, except to the airport for the flight to Vegas, and I guess the country hick had lost her protective coating. Buckthorn was only 200 miles away, but still I felt as though I'd arrived on a train in the middle of the night after three days of travel and didn't speak the language.

When Honey hadn't shown by 11 I booked a room and left

a message with the overnight clerk. I bought a newspaper and cough drops at the hotel gift shop and exchanged pleasantries with the cashier.

When I told her I'd driven down from Buckthorn she whistled and said, "Well, that's quite a situation up north of you." She nodded at the paper under my arm. "'All the news that's shit to print,' isn't that what they say in the news racket?" As I gazed at the paper, she rang up the purchases and continued. "I just don't understand anything anymore. All the drugs and booze, the lost jobs, people ripping each other off — and worse. The house three doors down from ours? It blew sky-high six weeks ago: drug lab in the rumpus room. Whatever happened to just falling asleep watching TV? Not that there's anything worth watching on TV since *Mary Tyler Moore* went off the air. Now it's just a bunch of idiots doing things that are *real*, so-called. And I mean, who the hell wants to know that much about reality . . . ?"

Up in the hotel room I laid the *Gazette* on the bed and stared at the article the cashier had referred to as *that situation up north of you*. I examined every individual word as if each one held a tiny compressed picture that would eventually lead to the gigantic irrefutable one. The whole time I kept thinking about what Honey had said: Fortune Bay was a hideous backwater that no one in their right mind would bother visiting in a million years. "You'd have to be lost," she said, in the days that followed our own reason for being there, "in order to find yourself standing at the edge of that gruesome fucking swamp."

Well, it seemed like the million-year time period had expired. Because the lost and crazy swamp people had returned to Fortune Bay:

BANKER DISCOVERED IN BAY

The body of Donald Phillip Aurbuck, manager of the downtown branch of the Commerce in Torrent, recently reported missing, was found in his submerged car on Thursday morning in Fortune Bay. A local couple found the silver MG in a remote but popular ice-fishing area on the bay and immediately notified the police.

"Dolores and I come out here a lot," said Mr. Henry Checkley of Cedarville. "You know, just trying to avoid the discomforts of civilization. Anywho, we thought maybe some jerk had ditched a bunch of auto parts, but then we saw the taillights and the MG emblem on the trunk. And that's when we knew there was a sharp little car down there under the ice. Sad. 'What a waste of a good sports car,' I told Dolores. But I didn't know about the guy stuffed inside when I made that comment. Or of course I never would have made it."

Although bank authorities remain tight-lipped, the *Gazette* has discovered that Aurbuck had been under investigation for misuse of customer funds and a number of other investment-related irregularities. When asked if the banker's death might have been suicide, Det. Brian Smith of the Torrent detachment said nothing was certain until the coroner's report but confirmed that the case is being handled as a homicide. The investigation continues. The murder weapon has not been found.

What the hell had we done with the gun? I couldn't for the life of me remember.

It was going on midnight when I decided to abandon the room and wait for her in the lounge. I had already called the desk twice to confirm she hadn't returned unseen and somehow missed my message. Not a chance. The same clerk had been on duty the full shift. Every time I called Honey, it went to voicemail. I asked her to call me right away, my words full of neutral yet ominous meaning, and hung up. I had just settled in at the same table by the window when a cab pulled up to the main entrance.

She got out.

Her hair, what was left of it, struck me first. It reminded me of the year she had a go at the Winona Ryder look after we watched *Girl, Interrupted* with Inez. But since when did an impulse to get a haircut come over her so suddenly? That's how I went about mine — just go in, make it happen, no fuss. But that wasn't Honey. And on top of that I could tell that she'd done the snipping herself, something she was skilled at from the old days when she cut Inez's locks on the stoop and they played rock tunes and made the whole thing into a lark, rather than the sad necessity it was.

She wore her banking armor, a gray skirt with a white shirt, and her pea coat over top. I was halfway out of my seat, and my skin, when I saw the guy and sat back down dizzy, like I'd walked into a familiar room and noticed a picture gone askew — the content correct but its scenic lake and forest tilting away.

He got out of the cab after her: heavy wool coat, laptop satchel under his arm, thirty-five or so, dark hair to the collar, and a pair of tortoiseshell glasses. As he leaned in to pay the driver, Honey waited, the cab's exhaust steaming all around them. That was the first odd thing: she waited. Honey never waited for anything, never mind a guy to hold the door. She would have gone on ahead, looked back, held the door for him, her coworker, and got on with things. But to stand there cooling her heels — real heels, part of the armor — in the twenty below?

If only hands weren't so damned expressive, and who knew this better than someone who spent her life hunkered down over a mass of oak and little bits of ivory, trying to wring a pleasing sound out of a bunch of wires and wool? But I understood this to my core because of her. As the cab drove away, they walked through the Melrose Hotel's main doors and into the foyer, she ahead of him, his hand on the small of her back all the way to the reception counter, then removed briefly to perform some dreary task, and back again. Twenty-seven bones in the human hand and wrist and I saw every one of them as I never would have, regardless of how many scales I'd run, if she hadn't taught me so many midnight lessons about nuance, intricacy, and bliss.

And that's how I knew that in spite of the suit and tie and those heavy eyeglasses: the hand on the small of Honey's back belonged to a woman, not a man.

I called her again as they stood waiting for the elevator together. I watched her slip her cell out of her pocket, stare at it (at me), and put it away again.

Four hours of blue-knuckle driving with no heat (it conked an hour into the trip home) and slowed to a walking pace as the highways closed behind me. And up ahead, the maniacal whirl of the snowplow's blue lights and the snapped necks of the ditched trucks bleeding gas into the snow as their wheels spun in the wind.

I couldn't help thinking what my mother would have to say about her prodigy now. And wasn't that her, sitting behind me in the shadows, her face drawn, her eyes filled with the grave apprehension of everything I'd done, everything my delinquent hands had been up to since our last day together? And what explanation? "Well, Mother, I've had quite a time since we last scrabbled together. Seems you were R-I-G-H-T on a few important points." How I missed her certainty at that moment and ached for the series of measured, aggravating questions she would ask in order to trace a route back to myself. Well, too L-A-T-E now.

Mile after mile, trillions of icy spears disguised as feathery holiday flakes charged the windshield, blinding me to everything but the white walls coming down — or were they rising up? — on either side of the car. And every now and then a highway exit to another faltering town appeared and offered up vague clues about when I might see something I understood again, if only the payday loan billboards on the outskirts of Buckthorn.

I stopped at a gas station for a container of windshield fluid (blue as my cheek in the rearview), a carton of milk, and two ham and cheese sandwiches, which lay unopened on the passenger seat the rest of the way home. Just before I pulled back into the storm my cell dinged: a text message from an unknown number with a video attached. At first I didn't know what I was looking at. It was recorded at night, so the quality was shit — but not shit enough: Havenhurst came into view, blurry on the tiny screen, but looming in my mind. The tall lights with the round globes along the entranceway, the empty concrete planters out front of the main doors. Whoever was behind the lens swung the view up to the top of the building, focused on Honey's lit fifth-floor apartment, then down again and around to the parking lot out back: two shadowy figures were at work in the twilight, laboring to lift the body of a bulky man into a tiny car. Our faces were obscured but the audio worked well enough. If you listened carefully you could hear Honey's voice say, "This fucking bastard won't fucking fit."

And what a voice. You couldn't hear that voice and not remember it. Meanwhile, I had lost mine. My mouth dried up. I cracked open the carton of milk. It seemed to have gone sour, or turned to ash. I sat there gripping the wheel at 10 and 2 as if I was still driving, careening around hairpin curves. It began to feel close in the car, too close, so I got out and squinted down the highway as though the Eldorado might appear out of the whirl of wind and snow, glide to a stop beside me and — then what? The window slides down and . . . nobody there — ghost Caddy to nowhere.

I got back in the car and called Honey four, five, ten times. Nothing. A caravan of truckers came steaming off the highway to fuel up and wait out the storm. Wasn't this the part where I ought to ditch the Chevy, swing my pack up into the cab of one of those monster diesels, and be gone? Me and Bobby McGee all the way to . . . But that just wasn't my role. My role was to sit there shaking, hit redial over and over, and feel like one of those anonymous voices so often, maybe *too* often, at the other end of Honey's phone: *I saw what you did, and I know . . .*

When I got home I couldn't sleep, but I couldn't endure anymore thoughts either. I washed down a couple of sleeping tablets with half a glass of whiskey and went to bed.

What torment, the smell of her hair on the pillow. I got up and wandered the suite. Then I crashed on the couch and lay torturing myself with thoughts about what she might be doing at that moment. For years after Honey had left I wondered what she was up to. Where in the world was she? Who were her friends? Was she sick, was she well? But I never wondered as deeply as in that one distilled moment at Havenhurst without her. And I found myself, for the first time, wishing for the return of the older, tortured days that were merely sad and unresolved, nothing like the savage territory of human emotion facing me at that moment — a landscape I never would have set out across if she hadn't kissed me, if she hadn't taken me to bed and put me through . . . what she might be putting somebody else through in some room (probably an upgrade) at the Melrose. How thoughts such as these could overwhelm all the other perils, I didn't know.

I finally fell asleep and didn't come to until early afternoon the next day. I might have slept longer, might never have woken up at all, for all I cared, if not for the hammering on the door.

14.

THE PROPERTY MANAGER INTRODUCED HIMSELF, a long last name, like a train hitched together with a bunch of vowels, and then got to the point: He wondered where the rent checks might be. He felt that he'd been more than fair with Ms. Ramone, but three months in arrears was the cut-off, and he'd told her as much.

I didn't understand this any more than all the other events of the last twenty-four hours, but it was the easiest thing in the world to solve in comparison. I wrote him out four checks at $950 a month and prayed they wouldn't bounce before I got to the bank. Before he left he said he'd noticed that Ms. Ramone often parked her car in front of the main doors and sometimes even propped the security door open. Both of these behaviors were against the rules because they contravened the safety ordinances and could I pass that information along when I next saw her — "as I have done myself many times," he added. I agreed, and quickly, because I was eager to get to the bank. But still, he stood there.

"So you'll tell her," he said. I assured him that I would. As soon as I saw her again I'd lay it on the line.

This got him halfway gone but he lingered. "One or two rules now and then is one thing," he said. "But so many, so often . . ."

I nodded. It was nothing, at this point, to convey a little empathy.

"Please tell her to stop breaking the rules."

Fifty grand was missing from the account holding my father's wrongful death settlement, on top of the $20,000 I'd loaned Honey. My father. What would he suggest I do in a situation like this? But of course he never would have imagined I'd find myself in this tangled neck of the woods. How could either of us have foreseen the results of his appointment with the Jeep, the drunk, and the Scarlet River Bridge? The only comment he'd ever made to me about money was a lecture on plutocrats brought on by a bratty remark I'd made about a schoolmate's funny teeth. "Nobody worries about cash more than people who have too much of it," he pointed out. "And that's why those who have too little are forced to make embarrassing, tragic choices such as whether to eat or keep their teeth. Let's not humiliate them further."

And what *I* stood there knowing was that no amount of money was worth anything without her, and that my father might have been one of the few people who wouldn't snicker at a sentiment like that, who would have slugged anyone who dared make a "poor you" joke at my expense. So yes, I wanted to break down right there in the bank and sob over the missing thousands, just like one of my dad's fat cats, because it reminded me how much I missed him, my mother — her.

I couldn't leave the bank right away, could barely walk. I had to sit down in the waiting area until my head stopped spinning and my heart regained its rhythm, or at least started limping along again. I stared at a wall of paintings executed by locals, amateur efforts that Honey never failed to make fun of: a stand of trees cresting a hill; branches of trees reaching out over water; three trees staring down at a fallen comrade. And then in a similar mood (maybe the same sad art therapist) but with watercraft this time: boats setting out in the morning; boats returning at dusk (but not *all* of them); a lichen-encrusted hull overturned and abandoned on the beach. When the receptionist asked if I was waiting for Banking or Insurance, I told her that I was taking a moment to enjoy the local art. "We have so many talented people in this little town," she said. I didn't disagree. I was too busy hearing the wise-crack Honey would have made, one of those perverse remarks that leave people twitchy and uncertain: *Too much talent, really. For such a small place.*

I drove home and called her again. Nothing. Voicemail was full. She was due to return that day, so I spent the rest of the afternoon, it seemed to me, picking out four bottles of wine. (Two French. Two Italian.) Took them home. Drank two. (One of each.) My cold was worse, so I swallowed a couple of cold tablets and had just drifted off when the phone rang. It was her, or at least her number. I said hello two, three times, each one more frantic than the last, before the line went dead. I called her back twice and then lay there for hours, it seemed to me, and could have sworn I didn't fall asleep, but then I woke the next morning to knocking. I assumed it was the property manager again and something had gone wrong with the checks. Maybe he'd gotten to the bank after me and all hell had broken loose in the accounts since then. Or maybe he'd recalled a few more rules Honey had smashed to smithereens.

I pulled on my robe and squinted through the security peephole.

The smell of menthol cough drops rushed in when I opened the door. He excused himself, turned away, and blew his nose. I imagined he'd caught a cold standing around in the weather out at Fortune Bay, fielding questions from the *Gazette* about the banker's condition, but for all I knew he might have caught it from me the first time he dropped by.

He wore a ski jacket this time, rather than an overcoat, unzipped, with one of those holiday sweaters underneath, a picture of a Christmas sock with *Naughty* knitted across it. When he saw me notice, he blushed and said something about it being an old gift from his wife. "She has a matching one. Of course hers says *Nice*," he said, and then got down to business.

He asked if I'd heard anything from Ms. Ramone. It crossed my mind to pour him a shot or two of Honey's bourbon, sit him down in the kitchen, and tell him a few things. Do I have a story for you! Aurbuck's shady bank activities; him assaulting Honey at the condo, if not the results; the lost week in Vegas; the missing fifty grand. Everything, almost. And even though I didn't have a clue what everything was myself, he'd help me figure it out. Because that was his job: finding things out. But that would include Fortune Bay and the MG. And wouldn't I have to show him the video too? So I clammed the fantasy up tight and said, simply, no. Would he like a cup of coffee? I was just thinking of making some.

He accepted, and we settled in at the kitchen table and exchanged a few general comments. Coldest winter since 1912. His two little girls had tunneled a fort in the ploughed snow at the foot of the driveway and insisted on him coming for tea every day at lunchtime. He asked if I had, by any chance, a Kleenex. I opened a new box and set it between us, which somehow reminded me of my mother and her well over fifty-minute therapy hour, but I restrained myself from inquiring, What's on your mind today? Because I already knew.

"Would you mind if I asked, Nicole, how long you've known Ms. Ramone?"

"Since the beginning," I said.

"Since the beginning of . . . ?"

It took me a minute to realize his confusion. "Oh, we've known each other since the beginning of time," I said. "Right back to lying side by side in our bassinettes over at Buckthorn General. Our mothers gave birth the same day." That was a lot of words. I reminded myself to be more careful, try to affect the usual tongue-tied demeanor I usually accomplished with ease.

"You've been friends all your lives," he said. "Or BFFs, as my kids would say." He smiled. I confirmed it. Not a peep about our nuptials in Vegas. Who the hell knew if that was even legal? Talk about crying in the chapel.

I expected him to bring out his notebook like last time and write down a few details, no matter how small, but no. He thought a moment. "It's unusual, in this day and age, to know someone since childhood."

"I guess so," I said.

"No one stays put anymore," he said. "Take this town as an example. There's nothing left for anyone here. Vineyards and B&Bs for the rich, that's the thing now." He said things weren't so different down in Torrent — nothing to rent, all the real estate too pricy to buy. He said it was one helluva situation and I couldn't help thinking of Honey's remark that day on the bench beside the cenotaph: *What a fucking situation!* Another one of those statements you just couldn't argue with. He dumped three teaspoons of sugar in his coffee, all the while talking about some kid he'd gone to school with and how they were still great friends, "like brothers."

"Of course, we haven't known each other as long as you and Ms. Ramone." He took a few long sips and added, "Still, I'd do anything for the guy." He set his cup back down and sighed. "You do things for family you just wouldn't do for anyone else."

When he asked if I had family in town, for some reason I found myself telling him about my parents' car accident — a distraction I suppose. I must have looked stricken because he reached out to touch my arm, and then thought better of it. He said people just didn't appreciate the privilege of driving anymore.

"Drunk drivers. The damned cell phones. All those bells and whistles. Pretty soon we'll have to ask our cars where they're taking us." Then he apologized, told me he was sorry to hear about my folks, and that he hoped to god the perpetrator had at least had his license taken away, though he doubted it. He finished his coffee and glanced at his watch.

As we stood at the door he asked if I'd heard about the banker up in Torrent. "You know — the snazzy sports car in Fortune Bay?" I admitted that I had.

"We're talking to as many of his business associates as possible. Let Ms. Ramone know, will you, that we'd still like that word with her? When she finally gets in touch?"

He shook a cough drop out of its package and offered one to me. Then he said that he and his wife had caught my show over at the Crescendo.

"You're good," he said. "My wife especially likes the way you do Bach's 'Minuet in G.'"

The next day I didn't know what else to do with myself so I decided to go back to the house on Montague Street: check the windows, look around, wander someplace familiar for an hour or so. It seemed I'd lost the knack for doing the very thing I'd perfected all my life: sitting still.

Our house was at the end of the crescent on a large lot, as I think I've said, the Carneys on the one side, bordered by Duvalle Street, and a few acres of leased cornfields with a row of weathered advertising placards on stilts. Every winter the Carneys fled to Arizona for the holiday season so Montague would be quieter than usual. This was especially nice because Al Carney replaced the leaf blower with his antiquated snowblower every winter — and there we went again.

I worried about having neglected the house over the past month. The water should have been turned off before the temperature dropped. I took the route I knew would be plowed, though all the roads in Buckthorn drove like rural in the winter: five or six feet of snow heaped on either side and the snow packed hard and slick, nuggets of salt scattered on top.

By then it was about 6 p.m. Montague Street had been cleared, but several feet of snow had fallen since I'd last visited the house so I parked on the road, picked my way up to the verandah, and then couldn't find my house key. I must have left it back at the condo, though I didn't remember removing it from my key ring. I swore, started down the steps, and then I remembered, turned back, and slipped a key out from under the old watering can. Good old Dad.

Something felt wrong as soon as I entered. I stood there for a few moments listening to the electric wall clock. It seemed that I couldn't un-hear the thing ever since that day in the kitchen with my mother. The sheet of plastic covering the lawn furniture rustled in the breeze. And then the usual sounds the old house gave off, groaning and sighing, like the rest of us, about having to endure another winter I suppose. But what was this different *thing* I sensed?

A breeze drifted through the house, the kind we felt only when the windows in my parents' bedroom were open or when the door to the mudroom at the back of the house had been left ajar. I heard a door close, and the draft died away. I walked down the hall and through the kitchen, into the dining room, thinking to secure the door out back. That's when I saw him.

He turned and faced me — a rangy guy in a windbreaker and one of those caps with earflaps. "Fuck," he said, then stood there a moment staring at me as if *I* was the intruder. Then he turned and fled out the back door. By the time I got my wits back, he'd descended the back steps and hustled off to the wooded area across from Duvalle. I sprinted down the steps and followed his prints through the woods and out to the side road beyond, arriving just in time to see a battered pickup swerve out onto the highway.

When I got back to the house I locked the door and checked all the rooms. My mother's office was messy as ever, stacks of books and assorted papers, but nothing seemed amiss; everything as I remembered. (Some thief, Honey would have said, he didn't steal your mother's bust of Carl Jung?) I switched on the light over the stove, locked up all the windows and doors, pocketed the house key, and waded back through the snow to my car all the while thinking about what Mr. Ear Flaps could have been doing skulking around my parents' house. Was he looking for cash to buy drugs, maybe? Yes, that was probably it. Always a risk when you left a house standing empty too long.

I got back in the Chevy and let it warm up — and then sat there at the foot of our driveway, my hands thrust between my knees to keep warm. I took a long look at the house, the woods, my mother's planters at the foot of the verandah. And I guess in what you might call a victory of wishful thinking over current troubling reality, I put the guy out of my mind and found myself longing to take the whole house with me — fold it down nice and neat like a pop-up house in a kids' book, tuck it under my arm, and off the two of us would go.

Crazy, right? But that's the only thought I could bear at the moment, because I couldn't handle facing another *why?*

15.

AS I GOT BACK TO HAVENHURST a call came in from Eddie, the manager at the Crescendo. The other piano player couldn't make it to work, stranded out in the sticks with a dead battery. He hated to ask but could I take the shift from 9 to midnight? The guy had always been good to me, found extra shifts whenever I needed them, so I agreed, and prayed like hell that Honey would be at the condo when I got home that night. I'd let up on calling her by then. She had talked about deking out of the meetings on Wednesday, now it was Friday. Part of me figured it was only a matter of how far away from Buckthorn she'd gotten, but still I couldn't let myself believe it.

So I drove to the casino, had a quick drink, and got to work. Halfway through my shift I couldn't recall anything I'd played and felt like I'd run out of desire (if only that had been true) and ideas.

So I had another drink. And you know that whole thing they say about drinkers feeling no pain? It's bullshit.

After the intermission there were eight or ten requests scattered around my tip jar. I worked my way through a bit of jazz, soul, mostly pop. One request for "Every Time We Say Goodbye," two for "Cry Me a River." I could have crooned those old standards in my sleep. There must have been a Bob Dylan fan in the house. I didn't sing many of his tunes, but screw it, I said (right into the mic, as it turned out) and gave them what they asked for: "Just Like a Woman." Halfway through I realized the obvious: the man had stolen that song from me. Every goddamn word was *mine*. In fact, it would never be that guy's fabulous fucking song — or woman — ever again. Because wasn't that me, standing in the rain? And didn't she know how to take just like a woman? And *make love* just like . . . ?

That's when I noticed the envelope next to my tip jar. I picked it up, a bit hefty for a request, but I did receive gifts from "admirers," everything from cash to fishing lures — and it *was* almost Christmas. I tore off the end and tipped the contents out.

It took me a moment to sober up and absorb what lay in my hand because all I could picture was Honey and me standing at Fortune Bay looking out over the ice, the snow blowing through the pines, her hands stuffed into her toque. The keys to Aurbuck's MG. I tossed them, as if they were hot, on top of the piano, and then grabbed them back again and slipped them into the waistband of my skirt. There was a request scrawled on a piece of paper too: *Crying Time*.

I'm not sure how long I sat there, my eyes drilling a hole in middle C, my hands curled up like a pair of cornered things trembling in my lap. In the hustle and commotion of the place — drinks ordered up, drunk fast and ordered again, the sound of all that hard-earned cash thrown away, the croupier's dreamy hands moving over the cards — everything faded away and I felt myself sitting in that purple twilight once again, starry pinpricks revolving over the walls and ceiling, soft light from the impossible chandelier obscuring the stains and disappointments and, well, raw fear of reality.

It wasn't until Eddie touched my shoulder — "What's up? How about another tune?" — that the room came rushing back, dragging my crazed inner mob with it: *You should be scared. Never more than now! Who else knew about the keys? No one! Are you sure? I thought I was! Something bad's going down. You're telling me!* And on and on.

"About that tune?" Eddie repeated. And all I knew was that I couldn't play the request. I wouldn't do it. I was halfway into a surprising discovery: nothing stirs anger more than fear — and too many drinks. I'd defy whoever was doing this, if only for the length of a song. At least, that's what I told that hysterical mob lighting torches in my head.

But in shitty reality? How could I have picked a tune that demolished myself more thoroughly than "I'd Rather Go Blind."

When I got home that night (the whole mental mob in tow, as if all the losers had piled in the Chevy and come home with me) I called her — and kept calling. I bounced the phone off the sofa a few times, poured myself a drink, called her again. It was about 2 a.m. when I decided I'd had enough. I'd call that cop back, as anyone would whose friend, lover — everything — had gone missing. Yes,

I'd tell him just how well we knew each other this time. The old thrift store hourglass caught my eye. I'd dragged it around with me since I was eighteen, Honey's pathetic stand-in I suppose, and barely saw it anymore. I snatched it up from where it sat among the bottles of bourbon and wine with every intention of smashing it against the wall. I remembered her laughing as she offered to show me how it worked that Christmas Eve at the old house: she must have thought I was an idiot even at eighteen, and it seemed I still was at twenty-four. But I couldn't do it, couldn't bear to turn myself into a ridiculous cliché on top of everything else: time runs out, that sort of thing. So I turned it over instead and watched the sand drain away while I drank whiskey — three shots to the hour.

A sort of emotional anarchy set in. Sure, if I talked to the detective I'd go to prison because I was an accessory to something horrible. But at least Honey and I would go live in the big house together. She could organize the social evenings. Or maybe the horrible thing could be explained and we'd get away with it. She killed Aurbuck in self-defense after all. The other stuff — she'd just have to tough it out, if it was that bad, and pay up. Because, Jesus Christ, this was the fucking limit — and for what? A shitload of dough that I would have gladly heaped on her with both hands? And all of this so she could disappear with some woman in clunky brogues and a dorky disguise? After what I'd been through with her? She'd better hope that woman was her lawyer and that her smarts exceeded her fashion sense.

I must have, for a moment, stepped out of myself, because that last thought struck me as it would have if Honey had been sitting on the sofa discussing this whole mess as if it were somebody else's plight. Fashion sense. That's the sort of remark she would have made herself about that anonymous woman, and then we would have laughed ourselves sick. "That suit! And my god, those glasses! What did she do, whittle them out of reindeer horns?" Jesus, yes, we would have laughed.

I couldn't sleep. I lay in bed staring at the fleeting shadows on the ceiling and remembered a certain night after we first moved in together. I'd worked late at the Crescendo and didn't get home until 2 a.m. All the way home I anticipated that moment when I lowered myself into bed beside her, you know, the way you slip into the lake off a dock for that last swim in September when the water's still summer-warm.

I could hear busyness in the kitchen before I came through the door, Ella Fitzgerald low in the background. And what was Honey up to? Slicing mushrooms. An old chef's apron tied on over her sweatpants and T: *Lou's Diner Open 24 Hours* embroidered over her left breast. She kissed me in the doorway and went straight back to the stove, chef knife in hand, as if it wasn't the middle of the night. As if nothing was strange. The butter hissed in that big, heavy pan she used for everything. I watched her hands move over the cutting board, slicing the mushrooms clean and thin, each layer a little sigh as it fell away from itself. The knife barely kissed the cutting board. She wore a silver cuff bracelet about two inches wide with an engraving of two sleek fish swimming in opposite directions, our birth sign. It slid toward her hand as she worked and settled in place again when she pushed back her hair. Why did a couple of inches of cool metal against her skin cause such turmoil in me, a fever I couldn't explain? But why even try to explain? I left it alone. It was enough to think about how, later, she'd slip the cuff off and set it on the table next to the bed. Unless she chose not to.

It didn't matter. She was beautiful, that's all I knew, and had been since the years of sparkle nail polish, and long before, further back than memory. But that night I do remember thinking, *Look what her hands are now.*

"Never crowd these guys," she said, as she placed the mushrooms in the pan. And then added an onion sliced so thin it more or less faded away. "Don't be stingy with the pepper. Because onions can dish it out, but they can also take it." A glass of wine stood by. She took a sip, passed it to me, and carried right on. She gave little cooking hints as she worked: Never use the jarred nutmeg because it's been through the mill. Smash the garlic and chop it rough. Don't overthink it.

Water started to boil in another pot and she dropped four pasta nests in. A cup of cream went into the big pan with the mushrooms, onion, nutmeg. "Stir it slow and lazy," she said. "But don't hover. Let up now and then. Let everybody wonder where you've gone." When the pasta was done: into the cream. Dusting of pecorino. Another splash of a nice Italian red. She laid out two plates, stripped off my coat, and tossed it on the sofa. The music changed and rose. "That Count Basie's for you, Nic. Aren't you glad the neighbors are always out?"

I pulled her pillow against me and inhaled the scent of her hair so deep I thought it would kill me. And then I cried myself to sleep.

The next morning I devoured the first real breakfast I'd eaten since The Egg & I in Vegas, and revisited the idea of calling that cop. But whenever I caught sight of those keys lying on the bedroom bureau I slammed on the brakes.

Then he called me instead. Could he come by for a quick chat? Twenty minutes. On a Saturday the weekend before Christmas? This was one keener cop. I suggested we might consider making it official: schedule a poker game once a week — an attempt to disarm him that I was certain he saw right through. He laughed anyway and dropped by about 11. We stood in the hall this time. No time for coffee it seemed, which at least might have precluded me breaking down and saying something fatal like, *We did it. Take me away. I'm ready.* But most of all *please find her.*

"Have you heard from Honey at all, Nicole?" he asked, this time tossing all formality aside.

"Not a peep," I said.

"Are you concerned?"

"She may be doing some Christmas shopping in Torrent. Buying a bunch of stuff she can't afford." I laughed.

"Sure, sure. You don't have to tell me about that. My wife's in Torrent shopping up a storm right now. I see another Christmas sweater in my future. But let me ask you this: isn't it unusual for her to be out of touch for so long, not even a phone call?"

"She once put me on hold for six years," I said, without thinking.

He thought about that for a moment. "I guess she might be feeling footloose and fancy free, what with no particular impetus to return to work."

"No?"

"I mean having left her position at the bank —" he drew his notebook from his pocket and flipped through some pages "— effective last week. I gather her final obligation was the year-end bank meetings in Torrent." He acted as if this news was understood between us, and I did too. Did he know more than he was letting on? It was all I could do not to request a flip through that notebook myself.

"I'm due somewhere else, so I won't keep you. Just one more thing," he said and handed me a photo.

"Is this person familiar to you?"

I took a good look at the photo. "No, not familiar to me at all." The guy in the picture was clean-cut, fifty-ish, thin. Nothing remarkable at all. I asked Smith if he was someone "wanted dead or alive," my feeble attempt to imply I hadn't a care in the world and what good fun, shooting the breeze with the law.

"I don't know how badly he may have been wanted alive, but someone certainly wanted him dead," he said. "Mind if I leave you this copy — his name's on the back — in case something comes up for you?"

"Why not?" I said. "Something to do with that . . . banker guy, is it?"

"Not possible to say at this point, but in police work, as in life, it's always a good idea to follow your hunches."

After he left I went online to try to find out what my cop's hunch might be. It turned out the dead guy in the photo was a local who lived up Port Union way, a jack of all trades who took tourists fishing and did some property caretaking on the side. His body had been found in a boat storage facility east of Echo Point, about fifteen miles from where he lived, summer and fall, on an old twenty-acre estate on Silk Lake.

But wasn't Aurbuck's family cottage the only one with that kind of acreage on Silk Lake? Didn't Honey mention a caretaker who taxied guests to the marina in one of those pricey mahogany boats Aurbuck owned? The news story hinted that he may have been killed by someone attempting to steal property. Stolen boats were big business in cottage country. Tow them away at night, sell them fast, and disappear. No connection made to "the prick" in the news story though.

I stared at the headshot some more. But it wasn't until I came across another photo of the same guy — standing in a woodlot, wearing a woodsmen cap and a pair of those canvas Carhartt overalls — that it clicked. That's when a new face began to take shape, like one of those old-time photographs dipped in a liquid bath where the image gradually floats into view.

I was ninety-eight percent sure it was the guy who had confronted me at the house. If I pictured him with a scruffy beard and a pissed off *fuck* on his lips the percentage shot straight to one hundred.

That night I had the worst dream ever about Honey. I would have sworn off sleep for good if I thought it would ever recur.

We were ten or twelve, lacing up our hockey skates in the hut at Crystal Bay. In reality there were always eight or nine kids in the cabin, throwing off their mitts and parkas, punching each other's shoulders. The scent of wet wool and smoke from the wood-burning stove hung in the air. People came and went from the sugar bush down the road at Blue Meadows, hockey sticks and snowshoes lined up against the snow fence while they ate maple syrup drizzled onto chunks of snow or sugary deep-fried dough and hot chocolate from the catering truck.

But in my dream the whole place lay deserted, just the white landscape, the lake smooth as deep blue glass, and six or seven raucous crows perched in the brittle trees, the sky gray and low. Honey and I were in the hut alone, lacing up our skates. She finished all her preparations first, as always: double knots on the laces, socks folded over the tops, toque jammed down over her ears — eager to be gone. She grabbed her stick, tossed the puck out the door, and threw herself onto the ice, her blades slicing tracks behind her. I may have been ten seconds behind. It was always the same: ten or twenty yards opened between us and she'd turn in one swift motion and either slap the puck back to me or send a perfect wrist shot to the sweet spot on my stick. And then off we'd race toward the marshy cove, full-tilt and playing every position along the way.

But not in my dream. Halfway across the expected distance she was no longer sprinting toward the frozen bull rushes ahead of me. She was behind me, under the ice. I raced back, ran more than skated, threw away my gloves, and fell to my knees, hammering with my fists until they bled. For a moment she stayed put, her expression calm, bemused, her eyes on mine as if staring through one of those old windows at our house, with the wavy glass and tiny bubbles caught in it. It reminded me of the day she made me kiss her through the screen door of the cottage at Serpentine River, before she let me in. And just when I thought it, she pressed her lips against the ice, her hands splayed on either side of her face, and I watched as the current slipped the whole length of her body past me and away.

What peace of mind after a dream like that? How could I shake it, stop seeing her face, her mouth, her body drift away while I skated and fell and skated and woke having never caught up to her?

Maybe it was this dream that got me wondering — was Honey on the run or was she missing?

I was ransacking the drawers, looking for Detective Smith's business card when my cell buzzed. A text came through with an attachment from the same anonymous number as before. And another video.

I decided not to open it. What if it was a graphic continuation of that whole Aurbuck situation behind Havenhurst; a kind of sequel that might take us out to Fortune Bay and I'd have to see myself doing . . . what I did. I sat there staring at the phone and picturing Honey (and me in the Chevy following behind), negotiating the icy side roads with her old boss and lover crammed into the back seat. What could be worse than that? And anyway, who was I kidding? Curiosity and worry always get the best of people; everybody knows that.

The new clip opened with a tight closeup of gold lettering, *Ebb Tide*, on a wood-grained background. Again, the atmosphere was muddy, half-lit, but when the camera pulled back the word's context became clear: the name on the stern of one of those fancy mahogany boats from the '50s, chrome everywhere, two-toned leather upholstery — a four-seater with a skull and crossbones mounted on the bow, the sort of craft that seems carved from a single piece of hardwood then hand-rubbed and lacquered to a high gloss. A dark inlay, lined with chrome, ran along the top and down the steep blade of the bow. The person shooting the clip savored the beauty and luxury of the craft's body — down the burnished sides and around to the two leather seats nestled in behind the flash of its curved windscreen.

The boat was stored on a trailer in a place the size of an airplane hangar, but even so, someone sat behind the wheel. He looked like he was cooling his heels and waiting to come into dock: none other than my home invader with his head tipped back, eyes wide, as if awed by something visible only to him, up in the rafters. And on his forehead a red speck no bigger than a fly. I had to look away. But not before seeing the note pinned to his chest: *How badly do you want your girlfriend back?*

I dropped Detective Smith's business card back in the drawer, all the while itching to — what is that thing he would have warned against? — take matters into my own hands. I began searching for Honey's gun. Why I don't know, because what would I do if I found it? The only weapon I'd ever owned was as an eight-year-old, a Supersoaker Blaster that shot water at unsuspecting opponents up to thirty-four feet — and I was too busy practicing scales to use it. And then it occurred to me that whoever this person was, they were, right at that moment, waiting for a response of some kind.

What should I say? I looked again at the face of the caretaker from Silk Lake and texted back, *Who are you, and what do you want?* Truly the central questions in life.

I heard nothing more until 11 that evening when, after I'd downed four or five shots of Honey's bourbon, they texted again: *$$$.* When I asked how much, they answered, *All of it.* I asked, *When?* They said, *Hurry.*

16.

FIRST IN LINE AT THE BANK the next morning, I asked to speak to Arch Kincaid, who had watched over my parents' accounts and "low-risk" investments for thirty years. He'd retired the previous month, so I got someone else, a guy named Aaron, who looked about fifteen but had a framed picture of a young boy and a dog on his desk so I guessed he was old enough to be seriously hooked up, if not married. I inquired about the ins and outs of withdrawing funds from the insurance payout. He adjusted his computer screen and asked me how much I had in mind. "All of it," I said, quoting the maniacal text.

When the account information appeared on his screen, he laughed and said, "Wouldn't that be great?" Then he waited for me to get serious. At least that was my impression.

"I'm serious," I said, and laughed too. "I don't mean cash, right on the spot; nothing like that. I don't want to leave the poor bank in tatters, or anything. Just a transfer into my account."

"How much of a transfer?" he asked, a little put off, I thought, by my "poor bank" remark. I looked again at the picture on his desk and realized the little boy was him, some years earlier, with said dog, a small, floppy-eared thing with an alarming underbite.

"Would there be a problem transferring the whole amount?"

"You *are* aware there's just over $750,000 in this account," he said. You'd have thought the transfer would require a fleet of armored cars and he'd have to load them himself.

"I guess I am," I said, with the reluctance of someone who never wanted to think about the insurance settlement, who had only ever thought of it in terms of my mother's life, except now Honey's life seemed to require it too, one way or another.

And what was all that cash supposed to do anyway? Bring me solace in exchange for the loss it symbolized? Sure, Honey and I bitched about being broke. But everybody was poor now, and what did we know about being rich? Why did I have to feel, at twenty-four, like some kind of obsolete loser because all I wanted was Honey and me together in the house on Montague Street, the two of us growing into old wrecks together while we tried to keep the wild lupines separate from the tomato vines in my mother's garden? Or we'd age and evolve beautifully like, what was it? — *those great Provençal rosés of Bandol.* And we'd never look back and wonder if we should have loved somebody else, somebody we regretted letting go of back in time, because we *were* each other's back in time.

"Ms. Hewett — Nicole — the bank can't transfer the balance into your personal account just yet," he said. "You can access

$50,000 on January 1st. Which is just around the corner, after all. And your mother has made arrangements for a consistent amount each month that would more than cover living expenses, I see you've written some checks on that already, but the full amount isn't available."

"Why not?"

"Because of the trust fund, of course."

Turns out, in late October my mother had gone to the bank and, before Arch Kincaid retired, opened a trust fund for me: $50,000 the year I turned twenty-five, increasing in yearly $10,000 increments until I turned thirty, at which point the whole amount reverted to me. It was a fantastic idea, entirely understandable, especially in light of what I'd done. She protected me to the end, even from myself. But at that moment I couldn't help thinking of Inez, sitting across from Aurbuck with the gun in her hand. *How much can we get with this?*

In the spirit of Honey's mother, I'd go home and scour the condo until I found that damn pistol, return the next day with a suitcase, and demand new terms. *Hand over the dough, you snarky pipsqueak or* — or what? I'd cringe, take aim, and stick a red dot on his forehead? I was too much my own mother's daughter for that.

Hurry, the text said. If some kind of lunatic had kidnapped Honey, how long would they wait? I'd expected her back on the 16th at the latest, and now it was the 21st. How patient could you expect a lunatic to be? Would $50,000 in the new year be okay? Would they wait until I turned thirty for the rest? I couldn't sit still, so that night, about 10, I set off driving.

I retraced a few of the routes my mother and I had driven in those last months and then, in order to pick up the pace and soothe the jitters, continued out to the main highway, stepped on it for about sixty miles, and cruised back slowly via County Rd. 8. I circled through town and headed out toward Motel Strip on the way back to Havenhurst.

Most of the motels were shuttered: Wigwam, Crystal Beachside Nook, the Driftwood Lodge. Only the Villa Capri had managed to make it through the years by offering weekly rentals to itinerant farm workers and then, after they drifted south, guys working the highways during winter storms. Its cracked neon sign flashed on and off as it had for fifty years; a lithe blonde woman in a red bathing suit diving over and over again into the darkness. The owner's TV screen flickered from a room somewhere in the back. I noticed a van parked at one end of the motel and an RV at the other, around the side next to a broken swing set.

Up ahead lay a section of old railroad track just before the intersection, now drifted over with snow. By the time I got there I was traveling so slow the tires caught for a second and set about whining and polishing the frozen metal. And in that second a commotion caught my eye around the side of the motel, like a gigantic wing lifting off in a gale. I rolled down the window as the tires released and looked back. A white tarp. And when it snapped back in the wind, there it was. I would have known one single taillight on the Eldorado anywhere — I would know it now, and all my life, and even at the end. It was parked at the back of the motel, acres of drifting snow and hacked-off cornstalks spread out behind.

I pulled off the road about a block farther down, next to the old train station, turned off the car, and tried to still the tremor in my hands. The RV was fancy and newish, lit by what might have been an old camp lantern turned down low. Was my blackmailer, and maybe worse, off in another car somewhere doing things I didn't want to know? If so, right then would be the time to charge in, slice through the rope that might have been cinched tight around Honey's wrists (at least I hoped so — a fucked-up wish, but the only truth I could stand), and drag her out of there. As I started to get out of the car, the RV door swung open. A few seconds passed before I caught my breath, pulled the door all but to, and switched off the car's interior light.

She stepped down, closed the door, and pulled on her toque as she walked across the lot toward the van, zipping her parka as she went. The door slid open, she reached in and took something out, and walked back to the RV. A bit of music drifted out onto the cold air and then dropped away as the RV door closed behind her.

Even though she was more or less the same height and build, and the Greyhound toque was unmistakable, I knew it wasn't Honey. Honey would have stopped to have a look at the sky, since she was free to do so, and wouldn't have bothered zipping the parka. Also, her jeans would have been barely scrunched into the tops of her boots. Honey Ramone, buccaneer.

I waited until the manager's lights went out (it was about 11:30 by then) and approached from the rear, next to the rusting swing set and the cornstalks whispering in the breeze. All the windows on the RV were tinted dark, but if I angled myself just right I could see, through the passenger door window, fragments of the interior, like little pieces of a flickering mosaic, which my eyes shifted this way and that in an attempt to assemble into something that made sense. Two washed-out letters over her left breast were all I needed to know she was wearing the shirt she'd bought at the marina the last summer we vacationed up at the river with my parents. I saw a portion of her hand raise a fragment of wine glass to the whole of her lips — and had to turn away and stare at the frozen ground for a few seconds. Wood smoke drifted past on the cold air and I realized the RV must have one of those tiny wood stoves popular with campers, hunters — and cold-blooded extortionists. When I looked back I realized it wasn't cards they were playing after all and heard myself whisper the incredibly stupid truth out loud.

I would have known the shuffle of those little hardwood tiles anywhere — and for a few seconds I could hardly hold it together while the old laugh or cry impulse set in, and I realized what a stupid joke life is and how much like a certain kind of movie. I couldn't help but picture myself old and washed-out and drawing my last breath with the name of that horrible board game on my lips (Honey's pronunciation) just like the old guy in *Citizen Kane*, except that his last thought was about something beautiful and lost. But then, so was mine — every night.

A camp hatchet leaned against the steps leading up to the door and I thought of pulling a "Here's Johnny!" but the hatchet was on the small side, and so was I. And who was I kidding? Even with everything she'd done, I still couldn't play her antagonist.

I walked back to the car, numb to the twenty below and oh-so casual, because who cared if anyone saw me? And anyway they were too busy picking locks to see anything but moolah and victory up ahead. I thought about how, if that woman in the brand-new mobile home had been the Honey I knew, I would call her up right then and there, and wouldn't we kill ourselves laughing when I laid out the whole scenario: how *my mother* had locked the insurance money into a trust and now *someone* was going to have a helluva time picking the bank's iron-clad pocket.

In the meantime? Someone could go on playing a dirty game by the cozy fire while — how had she put it? — the only one who matters in this godawful world sat outside in her dad's old Chevy on the coldest night since 1912.

17.

THE NEXT MORNING, I TOOK A CAB to the foot of Duvalle Street and made my way to the rear entrance of the house through assorted backyards. It was only a matter of time before Detective Smith, or someone, decided to knock on the door at Havenhurst, and what was there left to say? I needed to think, a bit of time and space with fewer traces of Honey, which in reality meant that I'd have to drink myself into a stupor and then slip into a coma. But a girl does what she can.

A few more text messages came in: *Deadline looming. Time's up. Don't fuck with me.* I didn't answer. Why bother with these insane games? I was afraid I'd respond with so much droll familiarity that Honey would realize they were busted, and then she'd be gone. I wasn't ready for that. I told myself this was because I hadn't yet come up with the perfect response to her betrayal, like the final twist in one of our favorite movies, the sort of thing that would nail her and redeem me. But the truth was I must have misread the movies, and my own heart, because there *was* no redemption or revenge. I just wasn't ready to see her go.

Two more irate texts arrived the following day, as I watched the backyard fill up with snow. I'd forgotten to store the patio set in the garage and the umbrella and chairs lay half-buried, a kind of polar beach complete with a few outdoor cushions tossed among the drifts. When I didn't respond to a third text, another video came in. By then my emotions were so eroded, my mood so, well, noir, I felt like making popcorn and inviting Honey and that femme fatale of hers over to watch the show. I played the part of the sap, of course.

The video was filmed in the RV out at the Villa Capri; a little corner of the diving woman's legs flashed in the dark and disappeared into the neon waves. They had decided, it seemed, to give me a tour of the domain, maybe by way of shoving that $50,000 RV in my face. I was ready to shut the video down, call Honey, and end the farce, when the camera continued along the windows, the banquette, the dining area, and down the hallway to a bedroom.

She sat with her back pressed against the bed's headboard. The camera caressed her body the same way it had the long, burnished length of the mahogany boat at the storage facility, emphasizing the fact that only with the eyes, or the lens, could you do such intimate things to someone without actually touching them.

I knew it was her in spite of the gloom and long before the closeup of her face because I was so familiar with every inch of her, although her hacked-off hair took my breath again. She was bound at the wrists and wore nothing but the Serpentine River T-shirt and a pair of underwear, her knees drawn up to her breasts. The other one had gagged her, no doubt with her consent. She didn't bother feigning a wild, terrorized expression. She knew I wouldn't buy that. Even her deception was polished in the sense that she knew to leave things rough, convey the opposite of what you might expect. No desperate, frightened loss of control and playing to the camera for her. Instead she looked into the camera's lens (my eyes), controlled, somber, and let her dry, parted lips say, without saying anything at all, *Jesus, Nic. Get me out of this.*

I turned off my cell, heartsick at the lengths she would go to hurt me, at what she would agree to do in order to fulfill their combined desires.

And then, just as quickly, I switched it back on again. Because a little flash of something had impressed itself on me, like when you close your eyes and the ghost of what you just saw remains intact for a few seconds before fading away. I tapped replay and endured the trip once again: her back to the headboard, knees drawn up, wrists bound in front of her, hands clasped together. My fingers zoomed in: the goddamn bowling pin wedding ring. *She's laughing at you*, whispered a voice from that gloomy inner mob of mine.

If I could have gotten my hands on the money I would have stuffed the whole lot into a garbage bag, driven over to the Capri, and dropped it at her feet; all so that I could look her in the eyes and tell her to take it all. Take it. Go stare at the empty sea. Kick back on your rose-colored beach without me. And then I'd give her a violent kiss and walk away.

On the other hand (and I know this will sound insane, or at least unsound) I had to stop myself from calling her and admitting I couldn't get the money, that she should get the hell out of

Buckthorn before it was too late. Love is strange, but memory's stranger. I just couldn't forget the two of us at age twelve, dancing to "Lover's Concerto" in my bedroom; at fourteen, lacing up our skates at Crystal Lake; her walking back into my life on the worst day I'd known; the naked weight of her the first time anyone had ever really touched me, the kind of touch I only ever wanted from her. There were moments when the reality of those memories swept everything else away — even that night at Fortune Bay with the MG. Even what she seemed to be doing to me at that moment. But then a thought crossed my mind like a shadow falling on snow when something silent and wild passes overhead, a fantasy as unacceptable to me as it was stirring: for a moment I was the woman in that dingy RV bedroom with Honey. I untied the gag and tossed it away but left the other ties in place. And then I drew her down beside me and, without saying a word, reviewed every lesson in persuasion, and restraint, and the most acute forms of pleasure that she'd ever taught me.

The next day, Christmas Eve, I got a black and white movie clip, two minutes and twenty-eight seconds spliced into the present straight out of the past. I could almost taste the rum we knocked back as kids while Inez lay passed out on the La-Z-Boy and Hitchcock's Mrs. Danvers tried to convince Rebecca to throw herself out the window into the sea: *You've nothing to live for, really, have you?* And tacked on the end, a text that said, *Deadline Xmas*. The girl was killing me. For a few seconds I thought of answering with Rebecca's own plea: *What have I done that you should hate me so?*

I had about $8,000 in my personal account and would have

offered it to them gladly if I'd thought it would end this thing once and for all, but I knew it wouldn't be enough because Honey, having had access to the account at the bank, knew what was at stake — we both knew what *all of it* meant. I had to get out of there, escape the phone for an hour and think, so I walked into town about 4 p.m. to try to clear my head. It was the first Christmas without my folks, and I needed the people, our little bit of last-minute consumerism, the lights, the local traffic, such as it was, in our little backwater.

Every year town council hoisted the same rickety *Holiday Greetings* banner over Main Street and installed red bows on the lamp posts along the boulevard. In the daytime it looked like the usual crappy impoverished street, but at night in a late December winter a kind of magic set in and everybody forgot the streets were crumbling, the stores closing, and how broke they were. For a little while everyone felt good no matter how close they were to the edge. Skaters in the park, the Salvation Army Santa with his bell, shoppers going into hock over gifts for their kids, everybody knocking off work early. So what if the whole devout thing had deteriorated into some kind of festive illusion. It was still transcendent in its own way: the night-time streets strung with blue, red, yellow lights, the carols issuing from the tinny speakers over the door at Robinson's. And after all there were still houses in Buckthorn where a few happy, shiny people went on living, even if they were just getting by, even if they drank too much and screwed up the words to "O Holy Night." My father said it was the reverence you brought to a song that counted. "The meaning of faith is your own to decide." I guess it was because I was thinking about him, and my mother, and the whole goddamn mess I had gotten myself into with Honey that

I got all teary at that moment, standing in the last of downtown Buckthorn in the snow. It choked me up how everyone was willing to go on believing, in spite of everything, that it still made sense to mix fancy drinks, shower people with gifts, and hang glitzy bulbs on trees.

He came up behind me as I stood staring at the motorized elves in Robinson's window, then apologized for startling me and asked if I had time for a hot chocolate. Was this guy kidding me? Because his invitation, when you considered the foundation, so to speak, of our relationship, struck me as the funniest, most innocent thing left in the world. How could I not accept?

We settled into a window seat at the Sugar Bowl and he ordered up two good old reliables and one of those flaky scones (a croissant) and asked if I wanted anything else. Then he went on a bit about last minute shopping and the kids at home, bouncing off the walls with excitement. This time, instead of the *Naughty* sweater, he wore a Rudolph tie clip his girls had given him the Christmas before. He said he looked forward to them becoming teenagers so they'd forbid him to ever wear it again, but meanwhile he showed me how the flashing nose worked, and turned it off again. We sipped our hot chocolate and sat looking out the window at the daubs of light from the street lamps and the cars coming and going, tires spinning in the Buckthorn slush.

For the first time, he didn't start by asking if I'd heard from Honey. My sense was that he was going over something in his mind, piecing things into place, reviewing for flaws. When he finally spoke it was as though he was talking to a trusted friend, or at least a decent listener.

He said there had been some new developments in "the Aurbuck thing." "Surprising developments," he said, reminders that you should never be shocked about the stuff human beings get up to. "I wouldn't ordinarily talk about such things before they hit the news, which they will tomorrow, but maybe you'd be interested in hearing a few details about the banker from Torrent."

"Okay," I said, eager in spite of myself. It seemed my caution had gone weak in the knees because of the festive magic of hot chocolate. If this kept up we'd be buying each other gifts.

"Because it seems that his past had come back to haunt that guy. There's a name for that, I think. You know, you do shitty stuff and pay for it later?"

"Karma," I said, thinking about Inez and her tea leaves, the old Ouija board.

"That's it — karma," he said. He gazed out at the skaters in the park while he bit into his croissant. He took a sip of hot chocolate, wiped his chin.

"This Aurbuck guy had done a fair number of nasty things — some financial, some personal — to an assortment of people and had some karma waiting in the wings, I guess you could say. Specifically, a woman named —" he slipped the notebook out of his pocket and flipped through a few pages, as if he didn't know every detail by heart "— Eva Lynch."

He looked up at me. My eyes offered nothing since I'd never heard the name before.

"One thing I've realized in my years on the force is that if you do enough bad things to enough people, pretty soon you end up doing something bad to the wrong person — and then look out." It was the sort of cautionary tale my mother would have told.

"See, this Eva Lynch person is a case in point, because Aurbuck had allegedly cheated her, and several others, out of thousands of dollars through a fake investment deal called Innisfree Vineyards, which is nothing more than a big fancy limestone entranceway in front of a few acres of scrub and brush up near Ergo Township. You know Ergo Township? East of Torrent?"

"Not really."

"No matter. The thing is this Aurbuck guy collected quite a pile of funds from lots of takers but when 2008 rolled around and the investment hadn't materialized, they wanted their money back, like everybody else in the universe."

"Well, my folks knew something about that," I said.

"Yes, a lot of folks do. And this includes Eva Lynch, who it seems this banker chap strung along for quite a few miles, I mean romantically as well as financially. He swindled her out of an inheritance along the way, putting on the dog at a pretty impressive cottage which clients like her were paying for and cruising his pals around the lakes in fancy boats she didn't realize she'd bought herself. Until she did. And then . . ." He looked at me and waited.

"Karma," I said.

"Bingo. Because it turned out that Lynch was what you might call a pretty unstable person and being swindled didn't improve things." He stuffed some more croissant into his mouth. Another gulp of hot chocolate. "By the way," he said, "why didn't you tell me about the break-in at your house?"

How the heck did this this guy know these things? He had to be the best neighborhood gossip of all time. I thought about lying (why quit then?) even though it was clear he knew all about it. I shrugged it off and lied to some degree. I told him I hadn't thought of it as a break-in.

"No? What's your definition of a break-in?"

"I guess when someone smashes a window, throws things around, fills up their van with your stuff. I figured it was somebody who wanted to steal something to sell for drugs."

"And you're certain nothing was stolen."

"Nothing that I could see."

"And nothing 'thrown around,' as you put it?"

"A bit of book and paper chaos in my mother's office, as always."

"Your mother was a therapist, I think?"

"Uh huh. So maybe the guy was looking for guidance." He got that droll look Honey and I often exchanged and then asked what made me think it was a guy.

"Isn't it usually?"

"Only sometimes. Sex, money, and death — the great levelers. But tell me something: do you still have the photograph I showed you the last time we met?"

"It's around somewhere."

"What if I told you that we discovered your personal banking information in that guy's car the night we found him with a bullet in his head, and that he was an associate of this woman Aurbuck swindled and ditched, Eva Lynch?"

What do you say to a jam-packed question like that? I just stared at him, reluctant, amazed, which was pretty much the only sensible answer. He said they had reason to believe Lynch may have hired that man, Ivan Haines, to break into the house on Montague, and then somewhere along the line she decided he was a liability, or simply no longer needed him. He made some remark about how that was when she promoted him to "captain of the ship" and described how they found his body in one of Aurbuck's fancy boats.

"Forgive the terrible humor," he said. "Sometimes stupid gags and ugly neckties are all a cop has. But bear with me for one more thing. We've been trying to locate Aurbuck's business partner in regards to a whole slew of irregularities at the bank. We found him two days ago out at the site of the bogus vineyard property. I'd rather not say how — you might say he was guarding the entranceway. Hard to know for sure, but it's possible that certain financial pressures might have taken their toll." He stuffed the rest of the croissant in his mouth, balled up his napkin, and dropped it on the plate.

And then he did ask about Honey after all — though we were back to "Ms. Ramone." He didn't wait for me to lie. He said he knew that she had worked with Aurbuck at one time, and he couldn't help thinking that Honey might have run across Ms. Lynch in her travels, though he sincerely hoped not.

"I have to tell you, I find Ms. Ramone's reluctance to appear, or even make contact, troubling. If I were you, I'd be itching to give her a good talking to when, and if, she turns up. Especially in light of your relationship."

He paused and looked at me carefully, a gentle half-smile on his face, and said, "Don't underestimate me, Nicole. I'm not as square as I look."

He put his notebook away and went through his pockets, found some change, and dropped a tip between our cups. He acknowledged that he'd disregarded certain protocols in speaking so frankly, and he should probably learn some discretion, but based on everything his office had learned it wouldn't surprise him if Ms. Ramone had her own pack of troubles with this Aurbuck character back in the day, and having learned a few things about how this guy used women, it probably wasn't lightweight stuff. He asked if she had been stressed before she disappeared. Had we received any odd communication or phone calls? Was there any reason, as far as I knew, that she could be blackmailed or coerced by someone?

"Anything at all that you wish to tell me?" he said. "I can be as good a listener as you." When I didn't answer he got up and buttoned his coat.

"Well, then, all I can do is run the numbers. And how I break it down is this: Ms. Ramone has either intentionally gone AWOL or she's missing. If the former, maybe she's joined up with a mentally deranged and desperate woman wanted on suspicion of two counts of murder. If, on the other hand, Ms. Ramone is truly missing, then she may have a whole different kind of trouble on her hands. And that seems to suggest that you do too."

He took another business card out of his wallet and set it down on the table in front of me, along with a picture.

"That's Eva Lynch," he said. "And here's my card, in case you've lost track of the other." The woman in the photo had pale blue eyes, striking in contrast to her dark collar-length hair, one of those shagged-out styles. It was a casual shot, a stunning northern lake in the background and a beer perched on the arm of one of those pricy teak patio loveseats. She was attractive, especially without those clunky tortoiseshell eyeglasses.

Before Detective Smith turned away, he said, "I couldn't help noticing that you're not wearing your ring."

I glanced at my hand. I'd left the "Love Me Tender" horseshoe ring back at Havenhurst on Honey's bureau, beside the keys to the wasted MG.

"Might not be the best time to stop packing a lucky horseshoe," he said.

18.

THE CLOCK ABOVE THE SUGAR BOWL's barista station seemed to triple in size, its hands lurching through the minutes like a clock on a tower, hammering each second home.

It started to snow. I waited until Det. Smith reached the intersection and turned the corner, then forced myself to linger another ten minutes. By the time I left the café it was snowing hard and the wind had picked up, gusting all the way down Broad and out through town to the corn fields and line of gray trees beyond. Shops starting closing, people got back on the road and made for home. My first thought was to grab a taxi to Havenhurst, pick up my car, and head out to Villa Capri, but Blue Angel cabs only had two cars left in Buckthorn and neither of them were in sight, so I started walking. *Deadline Xmas.* Did Lynch's demand mean one minute after midnight and no promises? Or did I have all day? The old hourglass lodged in my mind, full of sifting snow.

It was about 6 p.m. and I hadn't dressed for the weather: a pair of sneakers, windbreaker, no gloves or hat. I had thought I'd be back at the house by then, pacing to and fro and imagining how I'd give Honey what she had coming, and then take it all back again. That video kept playing through my mind: her all trussed up on the bed in the RV, that expression in her eyes. Two blocks away I saw a cab parked outside the 7/11, motor running, roof light on. The driver was inside buying a package of cigarettes and yakking with the cashier. When I asked him if he could take me out to Havenhurst he said the roads were closed until morning. "How about Villa Capri?" I said. Same thing. He was sticking to fares in town because his tires were crap. I thanked him, went back outside, got in his cab, and drove away.

He was right about the tires. I slid into a post box, threw the cab into reverse, and charged off again, fishtailing and sliding all the way to motel row, slowing only when the Capri's diver in her red bathing suit came into sight, the snow falling into her little patch of neon waves.

I tucked myself in next to the old railway station as before and waited for the RV to surrender some secret, a shred of information that might help me know what to think, or do, and when to do it. Shadows moved around inside, barely discernible against the venetian blinds. Snow fell heavy and fast on the windshield and built until it was half-dark inside the cab, blocking out the ruin of the train station, the torn-up tracks and rusted rail cars. The Capri's neon pulsed against the crust of snow: red, yellow, blue. I let it build, then touched the wipers and swept it away.

About half an hour later, the door of the RV opened. What if Honey stepped out of the trailer? That would mean that she had the freedom to come and go — and hadn't gone.

But it wasn't her.

She walked around to the side of the RV, opened an outside hatch of some sort, and searched around. She wore no overcoat, no toque this time — just jeans and a hoodie. She pulled the hood over her hair and bent down to sort through the contents of the compartment and then straightened up, something in her hand. And then, just as I rolled the window a few inches down to get a better look, the taxi's radio flared in the silence: the dispatcher trying to locate my driver, or my driver attempting to find his stolen car. I sank down in the seat, reached forward, and switched it off. She gazed through the falling snow for five, seven, nine seconds. Just then the wind rose and rattled the swing set behind the trailer, a sharp tear in the night's hush. She turned and walked back to the RV, stepped in, and closed the door.

An hour later nothing had changed: lights still on, quiet inside. I reached into my pocket to check my cell and remembered that I'd left it at home, trying to get away from the madness. And now there I sat twenty yards from that madness and Honey couldn't reach me if she wanted to, and maybe she did. It crossed my mind to pull up to the door, tap the horn, and inquire if anyone had ordered a taxi. While I chatted up the woman who'd gone over the deep end, Honey could slip out through the bathroom window, because isn't that how it works? But what if it didn't? No sign of life in the motel manager's office. He'd probably made a beeline for home when the storm began, so there'd be no assistance there.

By 11 p.m. I couldn't feel my fingertips. Whenever the video of Honey, gagged and tied, started rolling through my mind I replaced it with something else: me and her in bed in Vegas, or a loop of the two of us through the years. I had just convinced myself to get out of the cab, go up to the door, grab that little camping hatchet, and damn the consequences when *tap*, *tap* on my driver window.

I rolled the window down enough to see his unshaven cheek, the Rudolph tie-clip, and smell the Fisherman's Friend lozenge on his breath.

"What's going on, Nicole?" he said.

He motioned me over, opened the door, and slipped in beside me.

An inch or two of snow encased the windshield once again and we sat there together as if in a diving bell at the bottom of the sea, the neon coral surging in the distance. He said that a very long and entirely frank chat was in order, but there wasn't time. He told me that he'd parked his car in front of Frank's Pawn Shop two blocks down, because that's what you do when you want to keep an eye on someone without their knowledge.

"At least two blocks away in front of an *active* business, even if it's closed, rather than draw attention to yourself by parking beside an abandoned station that hasn't seen a train in twenty years. You're lucky, color-wise, that it's Blue Angel and not Yellow Cab." All of this was said in an eerily familiar tone. Who was this guy anyway? Had my mother somehow gotten to him before she died and made him promise with a capital P: never let her tough love die?

"Here, put these on," he said and handed me his gloves.

We stared at the RV.

"I know it's pointless to tell you to get out of the taxi and walk back to my car, so I won't waste our time on that. I guess you know that's Eva Lynch inside."

"I do now," I said.

"And that's Ms. Ramone in there with her, isn't it?" I didn't have to say a thing. For the first time in all our exchanges I let my unguarded face answer for me. He sat back and took his cell phone out of his pocket — except it wasn't his, it was mine.

"You received another video," he said and apologized for having to expropriate the phone. He said the video had come in an hour ago — and he didn't like what it told him. He pulled his cuff down and flashed the light on his watch.

"What *about* the video?"

He didn't answer. I asked again and reached for the phone. He shifted it to his other hand and into his pocket.

"I know you've been to the bank, Nicole. And I know Eva Lynch is blackmailing you — maybe the two of you. I may even know why."

"Give me that phone," I said.

He turned in his seat to face me.

"Listen carefully, because in about four minutes I'm going to get out, walk around the back of the RV, tuck myself in, and wait there. I want you to back out and drive the cab around the block to the main entrance of the Capri, and then straight up to the trailer, headlights facing the door. Nicole, are you listening?"

All I could manage was a nod.

"Leave the motor running and tap the horn, as if you were picking up a fare. She'll look out the window to see who it is and assume you've gotten the wrong address. I'll be standing to the left of the trailer door, in the shadows. Honk again — and again, if necessary, until she opens up and tells you to go fuck yourself." He gave me a small smile. "Then I want you to switch the headlights on bright and leave them on. You must do this before she goes back in, while her eyes are on the cab, on you, so the brights will blind her long enough for me to approach from behind. That's vital." He said we didn't have much time. "Can you do it?" He saw I couldn't get my mind off the video and took my hand.

"Look at me," he said. "Things have gotten serious, but maybe they haven't gone too far. Now's the time to find your moxie. Because I have a feeling both you and Honey have that in droves, though it may have gone off the rails somewhere along the line. Are you with me?"

"All the way."

"I knew you would be."

He opened the door and got out. "Wait until I'm there."

I watched him pass through the shadows along the Capri's perimeter, behind the swing set, and conceal himself next to the steps leading up to the RV's door, then I started the cab and backed slowly out of the lot, down the length of the train station, past his car, shifted into drive, and continued around the block, skidding and sliding all the way. My watch said it was about five minutes to midnight and I realized that the last video from Lynch, whatever else it showed, must have included the answer to my worry about the deadline: did I have until midnight, or all of Christmas Day? Now I knew.

I drove into the Villa Capri's lot, past the neon sign, and continued along the row of empty units, snow drifting in webs across their windows. When I reached the RV I turned and parked so that the headlights faced the door, as Smith had directed, and tapped the horn. He gestured from the shadows: *again, and harder.* The wipers seemed to beat in time with the neon, as if the taxi had been wired into the works somewhere. I leaned on the horn. When the door didn't open, Smith stepped out of the shadows, gun in hand. He drew his hand across his throat — *kill the lights* — and moved toward the entranceway and up the steps to the door.

She appeared as suddenly as he had himself, as if assembled from nothing out of the blowing snow, and approached him from behind. And then the hatchet in her hand got wired into the works too and flashed under the neon's yellow, blue, red. When she flailed at him with the axe he fell backwards down the steps, tried to get up, then lay still. She turned and came toward me. Just as she reached the car I switched the brights back on and she stood there in the glare, her arm shielding her eyes, the weapon raised. On she came, and then stopped and stood for a few seconds — and collapsed across the hood of the car, her blood seeping into the freshly fallen snow. At first I didn't understand. I never heard the gun.

I ran to Smith and crouched over him. The Rudolph tie clip came to life and flashed crazily at his chest. I pulled the cell from his pocket, called 9-1-1, and then up the RV steps and down the hall into the bedroom. I didn't think anything could be eerier than the chaos I imagined, but the RV's interior was neat and tidy, obsessively so — not like Honey at all. Only the bedroom was in disarray, and down the darkened passageway — a hellish banging, like someone trying to break through the wall with a sledge hammer. For a few seconds I convinced myself that I'd see Honey standing there, wild-eyed, hauling back to strike another blow. And I'd take the hammer from her hands and tell her, *You can let go now. No, really. It's over.*

And suddenly it *was* over — in all the wrong ways. Because she wasn't there. An emergency exit window had been pushed away and set about crashing in the wind — nothing but acres of white, windswept fields spread out beyond; the pure, virgin snow of Buckthorn County. Not a track in sight.

They scoured the RV the next morning. It was clear Honey had been there for days after the bank meetings in Torrent. The T-shirt she had worn in the video lay on the floor in a tangle of bloody sheets next to the bed. The police began to conjecture that when things started to heat up, Lynch got rid of her and continued with the charade. "Ceased to have need of her," Detective Smith might have said, if he hadn't been lying unconscious over at Buckthorn General.

The news reports said that when they searched Lynch's van they found a wardrobe of expensive outfits, men's, women's, custom most of it, all lined up on hangers or folded neatly into storage drawers. Maybe this was the sum of what remained after Aurbuck decimated her inheritance, the useless trappings of the life she was forced to shed.

I knew there might be trouble when Smith came to, because he would have seen the cell phone video of Honey and me doing that craziness behind Havenhurst. I was surprised I hadn't already been arrested and expected as much all along. But she was gone, so what did it matter? I'd just wait for whatever might come.

Christmas passed into the new year. I lost track of time and began taking long drives searching for a sign of some kind. Sometimes

I parked and looked out over the abandoned golf course next to Havenhurst, its tattered flags snapping in the wind. The parking lot remained empty, the whole building dark except for the subterranean light in the foyer.

Other times I drove to motel row and sat staring at the Eldorado out back of the Capri: long, slim, and silver — streaks of snow across its hood and drifts up past the rocker panels. Before the police dragged it off to the compound I had a look inside. Inez's old cassettes cluttered the dash, as ever. Old paper cups lay scattered on the floor. The keys were in the ignition so I slipped behind the wheel and gave them a try: a click and then nothing. Even so there was a certain defiance in its silence, as though the moment I turned my back it would rumble to life and begin its charge across the field and lift off into the winter sky. I liked that thought and returned to it often.

I drove up to Crystal Lake once, but never again. I saw her in the woods everywhere — concealed in the brush, her body found in early spring. Or worst of all, her pale face under the ice, her body slipping away into the frozen depths of the lake, my terrible dream come true. Each time I got back to Montague Street I worried that I'd missed her while I was wandering.

That's why I decided not to leave the house, ever again. Because with my luck she'd come straggling back from some abandoned cottage up north and toss a handful of pebbles at my bedroom window, all dappled with moonlight like in some movie, and the projector would break down mid-scene, and the victory music grind to a stop, because I missed my cue — off somewhere scouring the countryside in the old Chevy.

I bought a few supplies in preparation for her return: bottles of wine, that bourbon she favored, a few groceries. All that gourmet stuff she went on about — cheese and pâté mostly, some caviar, as if I knew anything. I even bought a pack of those cigarettes she liked in memory of that night up on Mt. Vista when she gave me that first dirty kiss of hers. I settled in, got into a routine: get up, play a little piano, look outside for tracks in the snow, go to bed. I'm not sure how long it took me to realize she wasn't coming back, that she'd never set foot on the verandah of the house on Montague Street again, not in winter, not spring, or any season at all.

There were mirrors in the house of course, and you'd think I would have seen myself in them, but if I did I didn't care. I never checked time or day, because I seemed to have developed uncanny insights into more important things. Time was stupid, for instance. And winter was wrongly maligned, because if you stepped outside naked it didn't take long to start feeling warm and even pleasantly lethargic. I must have had a few baths but can't be sure. One day I smoked a few cigarettes and thought about cutting my hair short like Honey's had been when I last saw her — but there was nothing, nothing in the world, like Honey the last time I saw her.

Now this is where it gets strange, because you see I thought that I went straight from the house to the mental health ward down in Torrent. It seemed to me that a guy from the electric company (that was the first time I saw my condition — in his eyes) came by to check the meter and got freaked out and called the cops, who called an ambulance. But I'm told it wasn't that way at all. Instead, the security guard at the police auto compound found me sitting in the Caddy sipping bourbon out of Honey's flask at 2:03 in the thirty below. And how I got there, and how it got to be February, I didn't know, and didn't care. And when he asked me what on earth I was doing there they say I told him, "Earth? I'm *leaving* earth. Stand away from the afterburners."

But that smacks of exaggeration if you ask me, just another swarm of blackflies and rumor; the sort of theatrical bullshit people make up because they live in towns where nothing ever happens.

19.

I DECIDED TO THINK OF MY TIME at the ward as a kind of enforced caesura, and me beating out the time like my father's old metronome. They certified me after the Eldorado episode because of my condition, but that really wasn't necessary because I didn't care where I was, or why, so hanging around with a bunch of disheveled, addicted euchre players was fine by me. They wouldn't catch me stepping across the line on the floor that separated the patients (inmates) from the great outdoors.

I gave music lessons, mostly for guitar, which I could play a little too in a pinch, and entertained the troops on Saturday nights after the double-feature. I became part of a little coven of women who were either coming down from drugs, kicking alcohol, or putting screwed-up relationships behind them. But some were just pale and sad and didn't know why. All were depressed, anxious — and really nice people. You'd almost be forgiven if you thought this might be one of their problems: they were too nice. But at the same time their various conditions made you believe it just isn't possible to be too nice to *anyone*. I don't know. I thought of them as another collection of folks, like the casino crowd, who had gambled and lost a rigged game, but there were differences: none of them bothered writing requests on a piece of paper and leaving them on the piano, an old Heintzman upright — they just shouted them out. Country, rhythm and blues, southern rock — whatever they wanted.

All the folks knew each other's business and weren't shy about offering opinions about my situation. They reminded me of a kind of unkempt ladies film club, a bunch of hyper-vigilant, rough-hewn critics who got together every Sunday to pop some corn and pick apart that month's offering. They took it personally, defending their point of view sometimes to the point of anxiety attacks.

Some of them (the realists) thought Honey had been the force behind the whole thing all along: she and Lynch had killed Aurbuck and I'd been seduced into their game for the insurance policy money, and then Lynch had to die when things started to close in; Honey couldn't risk her being caught and spilling the beans. They were amazed I couldn't see that and worried about how I'd make out in the world once I pulled myself together and got released.

The majority (romantics) were sure that Honey and I had both been blackmailed from the start, that Eva Lynch — jilted, swindled, and broke — had Aurbuck trailed by the guy from Silk Lake. The scene behind Havenhurst was a gift to Lynch. She forced Honey to steal the fifty grand and ask for more, or she'd send the video to the cops, or kill us both. To spare my feelings, my coven stopped short of conjecturing about what had happened to Honey, although I could see the awful scene in their eyes.

I never did see the video Detective Smith refused to show me that night, but his words, the expression on his face, were enough. I didn't care which scenario was true. I just wanted Honey to be alive somewhere, anywhere. I pictured her lying in bed (alone) in a room by the sea or strolling a beach, a sack of seashells dangling from one hand, a glass of one of those *idiosyncratic rosés from Abruzzo* in the other. The original girl from Ipanema or Tuscany — or wherever there was a curve of sea so clear that its boats seem suspended on air, their shadows stretched out on the pale sand below.

On the other hand if that's where she was, without me, I couldn't help hating her all over again, just as I had when she vanished from Buckthorn at eighteen. And when that happened I reminded myself of poor Johnny Farrell in *Gilda*, which is a fucked-up role to get stuck with — being so in touch with those rotten, wrung-out feelings and no one there to be stung by your bitter repartee.

Jealousy. What torture. It's like getting hung up on barbed wire somewhere deep inside yourself.

Detective Smith, after he recovered, visited me a couple of times at the ward and made an appearance the day I got out. I think he assumed I might be worried about some sort of blowback, that I might be found complicit in some way in the death of Aurbuck and maybe even Eva Lynch. And yes, I felt guilty, but I didn't really care what happened to me. Still he went out of his way to suggest that, in his view, the only thing I had been guilty of was being a half-assed sleuth trying to make sense of her own blackmail. On top of that I had saved a policeman's life, he said — the 9-1-1 call, which I thought anyone would have made, and my attempt to stop his bleeding from Lynch's attack. But how could I have done otherwise when he reminded me so much of my mother?

As for the compromising video, the voice was, perhaps, Honey's, but was the other figure me? Wasn't it just as likely that it was Eva Lynch? The whole mystery was inconclusive unless I confessed, and although I didn't really care about living anymore I especially didn't want to feel that way while in prison, where someone might rescue me if reality became too much.

At our last meeting he asked me, "Just out of curiosity, did Honey happen to own a gun?" When I didn't answer — it seemed I couldn't stop being cagey — he said the whole thing was curious because it wasn't a bullet from his own police revolver that took Eva Lynch down, as even he (dazed and half-dead) had thought at first.

"It was from an old Browning pistol that we traced back to a gas station robbery in Buckthorn County forty-three years ago. Almost certainly the same gun that killed Aurbuck."

I thought of spilling the whole thing right then and there. He might have enjoyed hearing about Inez trying to hold up Aurbuck for a loan. But if I did, he'd have to fill out a report, and one thing would lead to the next, and the facts might start interfering with the truth. He didn't press, I stayed neutral: our usual agreement.

"Curious," he said.

Before we parted he asked if I'd sprung the Caddy from the police compound. "Long gone," I said. "Given to the guy whose cab I stole and dented up pretty badly the night we — went looking for Honey."

The cabbie had told me that he planned to mount a light on top and swan the summer tourists around in style, but we both knew that would never be. No one bothers with cabs in Buckthorn anymore unless they're looking for a cruise back into the "happy golden days of yore," which apparently never happened anyway. But you can't go by me.

As I said, I promised myself I'd never go back to the house on Montague Street — afraid of what I'd find there: 2,000 square feet of nothing, the limbs of the giant maples heavy on the ground, the birches jumpy in the ruined wind, my father's guitar unstrung on the porch. But it turned out that whether I chose to return or not was beside the point — because it was as if that house had been waiting for the developer (or the guy from Pottery Barn) to throw open the gate — and then it shed its skin like a living thing and escaped the spot where it had stood for over a century. It drifted around until it found me, and now it's become some kind of willful thing I'll never be free of, nudging me from behind and gone when I turn around. I see now that me and the house are stuck with each other, the two of us inhabited by the absence of each one of them — all my missing.

Another few months go by and still my setlist hadn't changed much since the Crescendo. Wherever I went, there was no shortage of people prepared to get misty over songs like "I Put a Spell on You" or "Someone to Watch Over Me" — anything that helped them latch onto a dignified reason for feeling bad, and then have it draw to a conclusion with the song, although I can't say it worked for me.

I'd be bullshitting if I said I didn't think about her all the time, especially at work when I allowed myself the rare indulgence of closing the set with "Lover's Concerto." I'd let myself get lost again, imagining my silly vignette, the one I described to Honey that last night at the Grand Hotel when I finally told her how much I loved her. I look up from the keyboard one night and the casino door opens — cue the sexy sax riff, the lazy ceiling fan, close in on the piano player's hands, wearing her luckless good luck ring . . . But as I said it was a ridiculous indulgence. Because that little dream is nothing more than a fantasy from a certain kind of movie known for its moody lighting and shiny nighttime streets: unhappy ending, nobody wins.

A few weeks ago I took a job at another casino. It doesn't matter where, by then they'd all become one single gambling hall, each one merging into the next, every town the same too, slightly larger or smaller, most of them failing. I added a few new songs — the same combo of pop and blues: "What's New," "On the Sentimental Side," "Since I Fell for You." I had to laugh at my overly sincere song list. Just like my old man, but I did a hell of a job; I'd gone from being a half-baked crooner to a vocalist and singer, it seemed, in spite of myself. I could go on about texture and color, a certain raw catch in the throat, but it was more than that. I'm not blowing my own cornet, because it's just another example of serendipity, or fate, if you like, and had nothing to do with me. It's just that Honey had taught me how to put a song together by breaking something in me. And now I was fit to understand what my father meant when he told me, "Master the instrument's rules. By all means be intentional and perfect. But then, when life —" I know now he meant love "— comes along and drags you to your knees, throw everything away — and get down to making music."

I always rented a room wherever I traveled rather than apartment or suite because I knew the time was limited before I'd set off again. A packet of forwarded mail caught up with me at the latest address, most of it bills that I'm embarrassed to say went unpaid for months because of nothing more than forgetfulness and neglect (my new philosophy). I sat down one night to make things right, got them all squared away, stamped and ready to mail at the post box in town. No online convenience for me. I had cut my cord to the world, I guess you could say — gone offline and barely used my cell phone. My plan was to become a piano playing hermit on the move, swept back into the past, maybe, but what did it matter? I only know I was halfway there.

The last piece of mail was one of those brown five-by-seven envelopes with a mess of colorful postage stamps: depictions of small dwellings, white and ochre, on a rocky cliff. Inside was a fold-out map showing a long stretch of coastline and a small island beside it, a ragged scrap of washed-out green, as if that's all that remained after being worn away by the sea. It had been circled two or three times with a blue marker, and then a quick sketch of a window with curtains lifting in the breeze. I could smell the salt air, the rosemary, and lemon trees.

I felt dizzy, then faint, like that day in the change room at Robinson's. I watched her hands tie back her hair, as if she was right there with me, and longed to press my lips to the little brass safety pin that held her bra strap together. And where should I run to regain my composure now? Back to an empty house on Montague Street in a town that no longer existed? Wouldn't it be just like me to doubt her secret sign, the very one I'd searched for everywhere, as if it was nothing more than another Honey-related rumor, someone's sick lie, and dig up some reason to stay put in my crumby life. But here's the thing: in all the times I'd lost her, I had never felt her absence as keenly as when I sat in the hotel room, staring at that little blue scrawl, and imagined finding her again.

So to hell with composure, and even self-control. I'd throw myself away, like I was meant to do from the start. I'd pack my banged-up suitcase and join her on that island of hers, with rose-colored sand or whatever it turned out to be. Who cared if it was nothing more than the half-assed dream of a woman who couldn't face up to the world's facts? I mean, who really can, if we're honest. Sometimes the truth is all we've got, even if we keep it to ourselves.

And didn't we agree to meet up later if we ever parted — some train station in the middle of nowhere, or a cabin up north with a dilapidated dock and a banged-up rowboat knocking alongside? Of course we did. We made the pact at eight, at thirteen, at twenty-four, and in the middle of every long night we spent together.

And I realize now that's just what my father promised my mother on her birthday every year as he clowned his way through that corny Aznavour tune, with nothing but aching candor for the last eight bars.

Acknowledgments

HEARTFELT THANKS to my agent, Samantha Haywood at Transatlantic Agency, and my editor, Jen Knoch at ECW Press. They are all the proof I need that Lady Luck smiled on me twice. How awesome of ECW Press to let *Honey* hang around their offices with all the cool and talented people. Thanks to the cast at ECW Press: Jessica Albert, Crissy Calhoun, Emily Ferko, Tania Blokhuis, Leah Kleynhans, and Laura Pastore.

I'm grateful to Barbara Pulling, Pearl Luke, Mona Fertig, Michelle Benjamin, and Shari Macdonald for valuable input.

Love to my sister, Barb Egerter, my brother, Mike Brooks, and my friend and business partner, Kim Nash, who helped me find the time to write this novel. Thanks to Michael Egerter for that inspiring postcard from the Rock & Roll Hall of Fame.

Some time ago, the family of my high school writing teacher, Judy Wilson-Bucknam, returned to me, after she died, a scrapbook of poems and photographs that I gave to her on the last day of school. I thank them for their kindness, and I remember her.

© SHARI MACDONALD

BRENDA BROOKS has published two poetry collections and a novel, *Gotta Find Me an Angel*, a finalist for the Amazon.ca/Books in Canada First Novel Award. She lives on Salt Spring Island, B.C.

At ECW Press, we want you to enjoy this book in whatever format you like, whenever you like. Leave your print book at home and take the eBook to go! Purchase the print edition and receive the eBook free. Just send an email to ebook@ecwpress.com and include:

- the book title
- the name of the store where you purchased it
- your receipt number
- your preference of file type: PDF or ePub

A real person will respond to your email with your eBook attached. And thanks for supporting an independently owned Canadian publisher with your purchase!